P9-DDS-539

Harlequin
Presents..

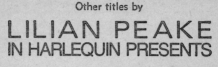

LILIAN PEAKE

till the end of time

HARLEQUIN BOOKS
toronto-winnipeg

Harlequin Presents edition published December 1975
SBN 373-70620-0

Original hard cover edition published in 1973
by Mills & Boon Limited

CHAPTER I

THE morning was overcast, the temperature low enough to make people draw in their shoulders and stamp their feet as they waited for buses to take them to work. The last day of the year seemed to be doing its best to prevent anyone from mourning its passing.

Marisa, washing her breakfast dishes, looked out of the kitchen window. The small back garden was littered with faded roses and summer left-overs like a tea table after a children's party. She chided herself again for her neglect.

There was a time when she had loved the garden. There was a time when life had had meaning and purpose, when every day had held a promise and a challenge like a piece of material waiting for the scissors to cut into it and shape it into a new dress.

At the end of the garden the car park – strictly temporary, the Council had warned – was filling up. Once houses had stood there, but they had been bulldozed into rubble and the rubble cleared and now the land was waiting to be developed.

The house Marisa lived in was small, old and one of a terrace of six. Four of the houses were empty and boarded up. The remaining two were occupied – hers and her next-door neighbours', Hester Worrell's and her son's. Mrs. Worrell, who owned the six houses which comprised the terrace, refused to sell.

All around them houses had been knocked down and in their place were buildings in the course of erection, offices mostly, giant blocks of concrete and glass, moving nearer, encroaching on their privacy, slowly, slowly winning. Mrs. Worrell knew they were winning, but still she would not sell.

People said, cynically, that she knew what she was about – the longer she delayed selling, the higher went the value of the land. But they were wrong. Hester Worrell, a widow, was not young – she had had her son Elwyn late in life – nor was she strong. She was a semi-invalid, more in bed than out of it, and her own

5

four walls, which had been hers since she had married many years before, were more dear to her than the large amount of money she knew she would get if she said "yes" to the Council's request that she should sell.

Mrs. Worrell had been good to Marisa, taking the place of her mother who had died just before Marisa had reached her teens. When her father had married again, his new wife had wanted to live her life with him unencumbered by his daughter. When Mrs. Worrell had offered Marisa a home, she had accepted gladly.

Marisa ran upstairs to apply a layer of powder and comb her hair. It was fair and she wore it parted in the centre and caught back by a slide, with two loose-hanging ringlets trained to fall in front of her ears. If she didn't hurry, she told her reflection, she would be late for work.

Everywhere she went in the house there were reminders of Dirk. There were two armchairs in the sitting-room; two chairs in the tiny room where they had eaten their meals; in the bathroom two towel rails, in the bedroom a double bed.

A half-filled bottle of aftershave lotion still stood, as it had for nearly three years now, on the dressing-table. She dusted it regularly and put it back. Now and then she told herself she would have to throw it away, but the day she did that she knew she would have given up hope.

She wondered what the passing of time had done to Dirk. She knew what it had done to her. The mirror told her, almost as if it had the powers of speech. Two lack-lustre eyes, blue and almond-shaped, looked back at her, a well-drawn mouth which had almost forgotten how to smile and an expression that was as bleak and overcast as the weather outside.

Every morning, before driving to work, Marisa called to see her neighbour. Sometimes Mrs. Worrell did not feel like getting up, so Marisa would shake her pillows and make her comfortable. Then she would wash the breakfast dishes which Elwyn had taken up to his mother on a tray. Sometimes Mrs. Worrell felt fit enough to venture downstairs – the pain from her arthritis varied in its intensity – and Marisa would help her dress. Then

6

Elwyn would come and escort her down to the sitting-room.

This morning Mrs. Worrell had decided to stay in bed. As Elwyn saw Marisa out, she reminded him of their date that evening at Jan and Neville Barclay's.

"It's not a party," Marisa told him, "it's just the four of us drinking in the New Year."

He nodded, saying he had not forgotten. His hair was so fair it was almost white, with a skin to match, so pale that people often asked him if he suffered from anaemia. He was of medium height. His eyes rarely registered emotion, being neither cold nor warm, his manner was pleasant with the merest trace of obsequiousness, probably instilled into him by the dictates of his occupation. He was twenty-five – only a few months younger than Marisa – and was manager of the local branch of a nationally-known men's wear firm.

Marisa drove her car into the all-day car park near her place of work and reversed into an empty space. As she locked the car and tried the doors, she wondered why she was taking such precautions. No one would want to steal her car, with its patches of rust on the wings, the worn carpets, and upholstery which was fast coming unstitched. But it had been the best she could afford. The maintenance allowance Dirk was paying monthly into her bank account had declined in value since they had decided upon the amount, with the help of a solicitor.

After Dirk had walked out on her, they had made their separation official. Without meeting again – the solicitor had acted for both of them – they had signed the deed agreeing to part. They still worked for the same firm of architects – Hilsby, Garner and Associates. When Dirk had asked the senior partner, Leonard Hilsby, for an immediate transfer south to the firm's Midlands branch, and had told him the reason why, Mr. Hilsby had granted the request at once.

Marisa worked for both Harris Garner and Leonard Hilsby, now nearing retirement. But Mr. Garner's output of letters and documents more than trebled those of the older man.

"I'm getting beyond it," Mr. Hilsby would say. "When you cease to tolerate the ideas of the young, it's time to pack up. I'm worked out, I don't get any more 'dynamic' new ideas. I'm bewildered by the youth of today, Mrs. Sterling," he had often said. "Their clothes, their music, their behaviour." He would shake his head. "The time's coming fast for me to get out."

Mr. Garner rang for Marisa almost as soon as she arrived. His manner was brusque and concise, never deviating from the point. It was unusual that morning that he allowed himself to grumble audibly about the amount of work which had been put on his desk. "Leonard might just as well have retired for all the work he does these days." Then realising he was not alone, he returned at once to the subject in hand.

Hilsby, Garner and Associates were larger than most architects' offices. They employed, besides architects of varying grades, consultant engineers, quantity surveyors and model makers. It was a thriving business with a number of provincial branches, and the firm had undertaken the design of many of the new buildings going up in the town.

After taking dictation from Mr. Garner, Marisa returned to the typists' office and sat down at her typewriter. Four or five other girls were at their desks hard at work. Jan Barclay, her friend, was standing in front of the office mirror combing her hair.

"Late again," she whispered, "but don't tell anyone. The car wouldn't start at first and Neville got frantic because he's got some urgent work on hand. I crept in the back way, while he, the privileged so-and-so, went bold as brass up the main staircase."

She started chatting about her private affairs until one of the architects put some specifications beside her, saying that should keep her quiet.

When Neville called into the office after work to collect Jan, he reminded Marisa about her date with them that evening.

When they had gone one of the other typists asked, "Going to welcome in the New Year in style?"

Marisa shrugged. "Just a few drinks."

One New Year was the same as any other nowadays. The changing of a number or two in the date, the hanging up of a new wall calendar meant nothing to her any more. Passing from December to January brought no alleviation of the pain, no lessening of the anguish whenever she thought about Dirk, no filling of the emptiness inside her.

She left the car outside her house. There was no garage to put it in, not even a sideway. The house was cold and smelled of damp. The Christmas decorations she had put up to brighten the place when she had entertained Elwyn and his mother during the brief Christmas holiday looked tarnished now, taunting her with her loneliness. She told herself she must remember to take them down before Twelfth Night.

Elwyn called for her, saying his aunt Florence, his mother's sister, was sitting with her till bedtime. He took Marisa's arm possessively and they walked side by side to his car. Marisa did not like his possessiveness. She thought of him more as a brother, having for years been brought up with him almost as a member of his family. But she did not repulse him. Could she be blamed, she often asked herself, for using him to fill the emptiness in her life, as a balm for her unhappiness, like a plaster applied to a wound? He had, after all, been the main cause of the breakdown of her marriage, so she felt justified in taking from him whatever he offered in the way of companionship.

Jan and Neville welcomed them warmly. A log fire roared in the grate, the lights on the Christmas tree had been switched on, glasses and bottles stood waiting. Floor-length tangerine velvet curtains had been drawn across the windows and the furniture was as modern as the house. Everything was in tune, the host and hostess in perfect accord. That their marriage was a complete success could not be doubted, and Marisa, standing outside in the emotional cold like a homeless person staring in the window at a happy family gathering, felt bereft and destitute.

Neville put on some records, handed round drinks, got out a chess board and played a game with Elwyn. Jan knitted and discussed office affairs with Marisa. Then she carried in the food and dispensed coffee and they talked the minutes away until midnight.

Neville poured out drinks again in readiness for the arrival of the New Year. He sat in an armchair and said casually to Marisa,

"Won't it feel strange having Dirk back in town?"

The blood drained from Marisa's face. The hand holding her glass became unsteady and Jan leaned forward to take it from her.

"Neville!" she reprimanded. "How could you? Poor Marisa, to break it to her so suddenly."

Her husband frowned uncertainly, looked from his wife to their guest, noted her state of shock and said, "I'm sorry, I thought it was common knowledge. I thought everyone knew Dirk was coming back."

Jan was angry with him. "You know darned well we've been keeping it quiet. The whole office decided not to breathe a word until —"

Marisa's colour returned slowly as the shock receded. "It's all right, Jan. Don't blame Neville. I had to know some time. But," to Neville, "why? And when?"

Neville looked at his wife for permission to answer. She nodded and he said, "Why? Well, you know old Hilsby's getting past it? Apparently Mr. Garner is feeling the strain and they've offered Dirk a partnership. When Mr. Hilsby goes, Dirk will presumably become one of the principals of the firm. And when? Any day, I understand."

Jan said, "Get Marisa another drink, dear. She looks as if she could do with it."

"But — but," Marisa stammered, "how am I going to be able to go on working there when Dirk comes back?"

"You'll have to leave," Elwyn said, his tone unusually sharp. "No question about it."

There he was with his possessiveness again. "I can't leave, Elwyn. It's my livelihood. Anyway, why should I? I've worked for them for years. Why should I be the one to be pushed out?"

"Well," said Neville, with a laugh that was intended to restore the lighter atmosphere, "you'll just have to pretend he's invisible."

"It's about time he released you," growled Elwyn.

Marisa answered dully, "He won't give me a divorce. I've

10

written and asked him via the solicitor. Apparently all Dirk said was that because we both agreed to a separation in the deed we signed, it ruled out a divorce unless we both consented, and he says 'no'. It's just a matter now of being patient until the necessary time has elapsed. He's sticking out for his rights, although what joy he gets from keeping me tied to him for another two years, heaven knows."

"Sadism, nothing more," Elwyn muttered.

"That's putting it a little strongly," said Neville, "but I do see your point – both of you."

Marisa stirred uneasily. Neville was getting it all wrong. If she were free, she would not marry Elwyn. But she couldn't get anyone to believe her, not even Elwyn himself.

"At least," said Jan brightly, watching the hands of the clock move closer to midnight, "with Dirk back again you'll have a chance to talk him round to your point of view, won't you?"

Midnight struck. They drank each other's health. "To the New Year," said Neville.

"To the New Year," they echoed.

"And," murmured Jan, raising her glass and looking at Marisa, "to whatever it may have in store for us all."

*

That night Marisa tossed and turned. "Dirk's coming back, Dirk's coming back," her tired brain told her repeatedly, like a hammer knocking a nail into a particularly hard wall. "What will he say? What will he do?" And would he release her now?

She could still hear the slam of the door the day he had walked out of her life. She had run after him and called him back. But he had not returned.

They had had a violent quarrel and it was, as usual, over Elwyn.

"He won't leave you alone," Dirk had stormed. "Always in and out, saying his mother wants you for this, and he wants you for that."

"It's only because I lived with them so long Mrs. Worrell looks on me as a daughter," she'd answered him.

11

"Yes," he had sneered, "and her son of course looks on you as a sister."

"When I think of all she's done for me . . ."

"And haven't you repaid her over the years, doing her cleaning, her washing, her shopping? And they still won't let you go."

"I'll never be able to repay the debt I owe her," she had cried. "You seem to forget we only got this house because Mrs. Worrell was kind enough to let us have it at a low rent, lower than any of the other tenants."

"I sometimes think that's the only reason you married me – to get a house of your own and the status marriage brings. You don't love me. You love that fool next door. You must do, the way you run in there at his beck and call. I suppose you didn't marry him because you didn't relish being lumbered with his mother all your married life. And another thing, you're *my* wife, yet you go in there every evening to 'attend to her' as you so euphemistically put it. What you should really say is to keep her son company."

She had cried, distressed by his mistrust and his misunderstanding, "But you're always working. You bring your work home, you never talk, you won't even let me watch television because you say it disturbs you."

"Of course I keep working," he had countered. "With you next door all the evening what else is there for me to do? Why aren't you honest and admit Elwyn's the attraction?"

"Because it's not true!" she had shouted back at him, maddened into losing control by his obtuseness, his inability to grasp her point of view. "I'm only human. I want a bit more out of life than sitting in an armchair, almost holding my breath in case I disrupt your train of thought, hardly daring to turn the page of a book in case I disturb you. Why can't we go out sometimes, like other couples?"

"So," he had sneered again, "you're dissatisfied with me as a husband?" She had grown frightened at his tone. There had been so many other quarrels on the same subject, but this was the worst of all. "You want someone more exciting, do you, someone who doesn't want to improve on his qualifications and

12

get promotion as I do, someone who gives you 'a good time', as they say? Right. Now I know exactly where I stand in your eyes, and in your life, the only thing for me to do is to get out. And quick."

That night he had packed his cases and left. She had not seen him again. It had been their second wedding aniversary.

Next morning, when Marisa called in to see Mrs. Worrell, she found her a little better. She helped her to dress and with the aid of a stick and Elwyn's arm, Mrs Worrell went downstairs.

"Don't forget tonight's rehearsal," Elwyn reminded her as she got in her car to drive to work.

"Are you word-perfect?" she asked with a smile, knowing that he could not possibly be because it was to be the first run-through of the play. He had been given the part of the leading man and she was to be the producer.

"I know the first line off by heart," he laughed as he waved her off.

Marisa took dictation from Mr. Hilsby that morning. He was in a talkative mood. He seemed to need companionship more than secretarial assistance. He dealt with two or three letters, then, with the obvious intention of delaying her departure – he was a gregarious, warm-hearted individual – he said, "All these youngsters coming up in the profession nowadays," was he referring in a roundabout way to Dirk? "I think they forget sometimes the fundamentals of design. They've got so many 'out of this world' ideas they've forgotten the basic necessities of architectural planning."

She closed her notebook and looked interested. How different he was from Mr. Garner who, with his impatient, abrupt manner, considered all digression a sin. "What these young chaps don't take into account," Mr. Hilsby went on, "is whether a building's properly planned for the purpose for which it was built. What they don't ask themselves is, are the journeys from one room to another too long? Are corridors too narrow for the job and cause 'traffic jams'? They put stairs in dark corners and they make windows too small. They design a beautiful wood-carved canopy over the entrance foyer of one public building I know, only to discover, when the building's finished, that it contravenes the fire regulations and down it all has to come!'"

Marisa laughed and took a quick look at her watch. Mr. Hilsby saw the action and with reluctance let her go. But he had to have the last word.

"What these young chaps don't know," he said, as she stood at the door, "is that a badly designed building can affect the people who work or live in it like a bad toothache." She laughed again. "It's true, you know," he said as she retreated. "They'll see," he added ominously, "they" presumably being Mr. Garner when Dirk came back.

She was typing Mr. Hilsby's letter when Greg Johnson, one of the junior architects, bearded, casual, strolled up to her desk. He tried, as he had done many times before, to make a date with her.

"Sorry," she said, "I've got a date already this evening – with a play."

He tutted and made a face. "I – er – did hear a rumour that a certain Mr. Dirk Sterling was returning to the fold. There wouldn't by any chance have been a great reconciliation scene, would there?"

"No."

"All right, I was only asking. Can't say I'm sorry. It means I can still keep trying my luck without an irate husband to punch me on the nose."

She forced a smile. "No harm in trying, Greg, but no's still the answer."

He shrugged and walked away.

"You look tired," said Jan over coffee. "Did we keep you too late last night?"

"No. Just couldn't sleep."

"Worrying about Dirk?"

Marisa nodded. She asked a little desperately, "What can I do, Jan?"

Jan shrugged. "Wait and see. What else? But I know how you feel, dear."

Marisa went to the first rehearsal in Elwyn's car. It was so cold in the hall they all kept their coats on, which did not help to create the atmosphere the play demanded. One of the girls called Sally laughed. Reading from the script she said, " 'Scene One. A sunny afternoon in midsummer.' My goodness, we're going to need all our imaginations to conjure up that sort of warmth."

She was the heroine to Elwyn's hero and she slipped her arm in his and huddled up to him. "Warm me up, Elwyn," she said.

He tolerated her hold and gave a lukewarm smile. Watching them, Marisa wondered how she was going to persuade Elwyn to show any feeling, let alone the passion required of the character he was portraying at the climax of the play. She knew him too well to fool herself into thinking he possessed any hidden depths.

They dragged chairs from the sides of the hall and sat in a semi-circle with Marisa facing them. They read through their parts, their voices echoing hollowly in the bare, shadowy building.

"Well, we've made a start," she said encouragingly at the end of the evening, "but we shall have to work on it, no doubt about that."

Elwyn took her home and left her on the doorstep. He gave her his usual goodnight kiss.

She took dictation from Mr. Garner next morning. Before he tackled the business of the day, he cleared his throat, looked at her over his half-glasses and said, "I don't know whether you're aware, Mrs. Sterling, of your husband's return here to Head Office?"

She answered yes, she had heard.

"He's written and told you?"

"No, Mr. Garner. There's been no communication between us since we parted, except through the solicitor."

"I see." He picked up a letter, scanned the contents and said, "It occurred to me that you might have become – reconciled?"

She shook her head. "There's no change in the situation between us."

15

He put the letter down. "It's just that when we suggested his transfer back here he made no objection." He paused, shrugged as if to say that such untidy things as broken marriages were beyond his comprehension and started work. He got through a considerable amount of correspondence, then looked at his watch and stopped suddenly, like an express train hitting the buffers. "I have to go."

He scraped back his chair and stood up. "That letter I've just given you, don't wait until the meeting is over, Mrs. Sterling. Bring it into the committee room for me to sign, then I want it dispatched immediately."

Marisa had her coffee while she typed Mr. Garner's correspondence, then, following his instructions, took the urgent letter upstairs and tapped on the committee room door. She went in. The man who was speaking – what he was saying was being listened to with intense concentration by his colleagues – looked up, stopped in mid-sentence, then went on talking as though nothing had happened.

The pause had only lasted a few seconds, but to Marisa it had seemed an eternity. The speaker, his clasped hands resting on the table, continued to talk. No one interrupted.

He was brown-haired, his face oval-shaped, his eyes intense and hard. He looked like a man who would not easily forgive a transgression and who pursued his objective relentlessly and to the bitter end, whatever the cost to himself – or to others. The man was Dirk Sterling.

CHAPTER II

MARISA pushed the letter she was holding in front of Mr. Garner, who took a pen from his top pocket, signed his name and handed the letter back. "Get it off at once, Mrs. Sterling," he said into the sudden silence.

She nodded and left the room. The discussion behind the closed door went on. She walked a few paces, then stopped. She had to wait for the world to stop reeling before she descended those stairs.

She hung on to the polished wood of the banisters – the offices occupied the whole of a large, rather old house – and slowly her head cleared. Dirk was back. And she had meant no more to him than a speck of dust on that table they were sitting round. Three years since he had seen her and she had merited no more than a swift, dispassionate glance.

"Don't tell me," said Jan, watching Marisa lower herself into her chair like an invalid racked with pain, "you've seen him."

Marisa nodded, her eyes blank.

"He's changed, hasn't he?" Jan commented.

"Changed? He's changed so much it frightens me." Her dull eyes swivelled to meet the compassion in Jan's. "What I want to know is, where do we go from here?"

All the morning she waited for Dirk to walk into the typists' office, but he did not come. During the afternoon she began to relax. Perhaps it would not be so difficult after all. She need never meet him, she supposed, except on the stairs or, as she had done that morning, at a meeting. He would have his own secretary. They need never address a word to each other. But the agony, her mind cried out, of knowing he was there, near enough to talk to, to touch, yet feeling his hatred of her reaching out from his eyes.

Greg Johnson strolled in, raising his hand to the other girls but making as usual for Marisa's desk. As soon as she saw him hovering, her hand closed over the pencil beside her typewriter. His hand closed over hers. "I know what you're after," she laughed. "My pencil. I know you architects. You get itchy fingers whenever you see a pencil!"

He bent down and rested his elbows on her desk, his hand still imprisoning hers. "So you know what I'm after, do you? It's not just your pencil, sweetie." He moved nearer. "Ever kissed a man with a beard? Come out with me tonight and try it. You might get hooked on it, you never know." He moved his mouth towards hers. "Come on, try it now. Testing, testing. . . ."

Someone cleared his throat. He was standing next to them and Greg straightened guiltily, turning uncharacteristically red when he saw who it was. "Hi, Dirk. You want me?"

"Not you. I want secretarial assistance."

"Sorry. Just fooling." He went on his way.

Marisa looked up into ice-cold eyes. Her heart was thumping so badly it almost made her body vibrate. "I was told by Mr Garner," Dirk Sterling said, his voice toneless, "that until I get a secretary of my own, I can use your services." He went on levelly, "I'm sorry I had to come at such an inopportune moment. Next time I'll take good care not to spoil such a touchingly romantic interlude."

Marisa let the sarcasm pass unchallenged. In the circumstances she could do little else.

Dirk went on, "I want this bill of quantities typed, and a dozen copies of this specification run off." He added, as he turned away, "Please."

"Yes –" What should she call him – Dirk, Mr Sterling? But that was ridiculous. He was her husband. "Yes," she repeated lamely.

Jan came in and saw her pale face. She asked, "Now what?"

"He's given me work to do."

"Did he say anything else?" She sounded eager. "Any chance of making it up?"

"Not a thing. He would have to come in while Greg was playing about trying to make me kiss him."

"But nobody takes Greg seriously."

18

"Obviously Dirk does. He now has me pigeonholed as a member of the permissive society."

"I wonder where he's living," Jan mused, getting down to work. "I'll get Neville to find out."

"It makes no difference to me where he's living. We might as well be at opposite ends of the earth for all the effect it will have on my life. We've been officially separated for three years and we're likely to remain so for the next fifty as far as I can see."

Soon after Marisa had typed the bill of quantities it was time to go home. She asked Jan if she knew where Dirk's office was.

"I think he's got the store room next to Mr. Hilsby's room. Later, Neville says, they'll find him a bigger office, Mr. Hilsby's probably, when he goes."

Marisa tapped on the door of the store room and was told to enter. The place had been cleared of a great deal of its contents, and a space created for a desk.

Dirk held out his hand for the work she had done, and took it without thanking her. "I'm sorry," she said, "but I couldn't get round to doing the specifications. Will the morning do?"

"It will have to, won't it?" he snapped.

"I'll stay late, if you like."

"No, thank you. I wouldn't dream of intruding on your private affairs by asking you to do overtime."

Words came into her mind, words that struggled to get themselves heard. "For heaven's sake," she wanted to say, "if we're going to work together, you'll have to change your attitude. I can't take your sarcasm every hour of the day. At least treat me as a human being. *I* didn't walk out on *you*. You're the one who broke up our marriage."

But all she said was "Goodnight," as she would have said to Mr. Garner or Mr. Hilsby.

He did not reply as they would have done.

Marisa decided that evening to take down the Christmas decorations. She could not stand the false air of festivity they gave to the house. She carried the step-stool into the sitting-room and reached up to the ceiling to pull out the drawing-pins. One by one she took down the chains and dropped them to the floor. She was stretching upwards to release the last of them when she heard a key turn in the lock. She froze. Besides herself, there was only one other person in the world who had the key to her front door. It was a sound that, day after day when Dirk had left her, she had listened for constantly. Now it filled her with panic.

Dirk stood in the doorway. "You can stop looking so horrified," he said. "I haven't come to claim restitution of conjugal rights."

She climbed down and made frantic efforts to clear away the mess, to sweep the decorations into a corner.

"I'm not a guest, either, so there's no need to tidy up."

She realised she had not spoken a word. "Why," she managed, "have you come?"

Without removing his coat, he threw himself into an arm chair. "To see my wife. To see how she's taking my reappearance on the scene. To see the house I used to live in with her. Is there a law against it?"

She said a little foolishly, "But we're separated. You shouldn't be here."

"We are still separated. In both mind and –" he looked her over and finished, with a touch of insult, "body."

Marisa was still standing. "Why don't you sit down?" he asked. "It's your home. It's not mine any longer."

"You've changed."

He leaned back his head and closed his eyes. "I have, haven't I? I've experienced a lot more – life since I left you."

She could think of nothing to say.

Dirk opened his eyes and raised his head. She could see the lines of fatigue on his face, making him look older than his thirty years. "And you?" he asked. "How's your love affair progressing?"

"Love affair? With whom?"

He got up and wandered round, stepping over the discarded decorations and picking up objects from the mantelpiece. "Don't pretend you don't know. Elwyn Worrell. Who else? Unless," he

20

turned and looked at her provocatively, "it's Greg Johnson?"

"It's neither." But she knew he did not deliver her by the cynicism in his eyes. "Why did you come back, Dirk?"

He didn't answer at first. He was looking at a framed photograph he had picked up from the mantelpiece. It was of the two of them on their wedding day. They had been asked by the photographer to gaze at each other and they had complied rapturously. He stared at it for a long time, then replaced it without comment.

"Why?" he replied to her question. "It's obvious, isn't it? What man with ambition could resist the call of a higher position and a higher salary? Besides, I missed the north of England. I missed the fells and the moors and the open spaces."

"But you knew very well I was still working here at Head Office. That's why you asked for a transfer away from it three years ago."

"You don't think I was going to let you stand in my way of promotion? If you don't like having me back, you know what you can do. Leave."

"How can you be so callous?"

"I'm not being callous. I'm merely speaking the truth."

She swallowed her pride and asked, "Would you like a cup of tea?"

"Yes, please."

She went along the hall and down three steps to the kitchen. As she made the tea and arranged the cups, she heard him wandering about upstairs. He opened the door of their bedroom and was in there for some time.

When he came down, she saw that he had removed his coat. She panicked again. How long did he intend to stay?

In the sitting-room he took the cup she offered him. She had to sit down now, to drink her tea.

"I suppose you realise," he said, "that you're living in a slum? Ironic, isn't it? Here am I, an architect, your husband, and this is the only real home you've known in years."

"Whatever it is now, it was a palace to me – once." She could

21

not tell him that it had been his presence that had made it so precious to her.

"Yes, that was all you really wanted, wasn't it? A roof of your own over your head. The only trouble was that to get it, you had to have me with it. Unfortunately for you, I got in the way – it didn't take me long to realise just how much. I was an expendable commodity, a redundant factor once I'd fulfilled my purpose of securing a home for you."

It was useless to remonstrate, to deny the truth of his statement. He would override her denials and accuse her of lying.

He stared up at the ceiling, now flaking with damp and neglect. "My God, how these surroundings used to depress me! I don't know how you can stand living here." He paused. "But of course I do. The proximity of beloved Elwyn no doubt does a great deal to mitigate the effect of the appalling conditions you're living in."

"Elwyn means nothing to me."

He greeted the statement with a cynical smile. "I suppose you know," he put down his cup and saucer and got up, standing with his back to the dying fire, "that these houses are coming down."

That brought her to life. "They aren't! Mrs. Worrell refuses to sell."

He smiled. "She'll be persuaded. There are ways. She'll see sense before she's much older. It's inevitable. Old houses – near-slums like these – are like weeds or bad teeth – they must be pulled out."

"But," she could not believe that he could be so unfeeling, "this was your home – our home – once. Doesn't it mean anything at all to you?"

He considered his answer. "I'm sorry, but I can't get sentimental over a slum."

Marisa tightened her lips and collected the empty cups. Was there no getting through to him? Where was the man she had married, the young, happy, warm-hearted man who had snatched as eagerly as she had at the chance of a home of his own, sharing it with the girl he had said he loved? What had it mattered, he had asked, kissing her, that they'd only known each other three months? They loved each other, didn't they? And that was a good enough foundation to make any marriage last.

So they had married. What Dirk hadn't bargained for, he had flung at her the day he walked out, was that he would be marrying their next-door neighbours as well.

He looked at the mess of decorations on the floor. "Did you have a good Christmas?"

"Yes, thank you." They might have been strangers talking at a bus stop.

"Did you spend it alone?"

"No. Mrs. Worrell and Elwyn came in."

His eyes narrowed. "I see. So you still live in each other's pockets?"

"Mrs. Worrell is a semi-invalid. She often can't tackle the ordinary everyday jobs, let alone prepare for something as special as Christmas."

"Does Elwyn still covet you?"

She flushed. "I don't know what you mean." She did, of course, only too well.

The phone rang. She panicked – it was almost certainly Elwyn. She didn't move.

"Aren't you going to answer it?" Dirk asked, noting her agitation. "Or would you rather I did?"

That made her move. She went into the hall and picked up the receiver. "Yes?" It was Elwyn. "Could you – could you ring later? I'm – well, I'm busy." Could he come round? She looked quickly at Dirk who was standing in the sitting-room doorway, smiling sarcastically. "No, no, you can't – I mean, don't come round. I'll ring you back." She replaced the phone and tried to find a valid, acceptable excuse for the call. "I'm producing a play. Elwyn's in it, that's why he phoned."

But Dirk was not listening. "So he's still at it? Which proves to me yet again how right I was to get out when I did. The only trouble is, from his point of view, that you're still tied to me. Too bad for him – and for you." He put on his coat. It was brown suede with a sheepskin lining and looked expensive. "He

23

may think he holds the winning hand, but he's wrong. I still hold the trump card!"

He went out, slamming the door behind him. Wearily Marisa went upstairs to comb her hair. She knew Elwyn would come in. As she stood at the dressing-table, her eyes searched automatically for the bottle of after-shave lotion. It was missing.

She bent down and picked the bottle from the waste paper basket. Dirk had emptied the contents down the sink in the bathroom and had thrown the bottle away. She felt a fierce mounting resentment against him as though he had destroyed one of her most cherished possessions. But of course it had not been hers. It had belonged to him, just as she had belonged to him.

He had drained her, too, of feelings, and thrown her away. Now there was nothing left inside her, not even hope. She was as empty – and as useless – as that bottle. She dropped it back amongst the rubbish.

Marisa called as usual on Mrs. Worrell the following morning and found her agitated and shocked.

"It's the letter," she explained, "the letter I've been dreading."

Elwyn looked grim. "Compulsory purchase. They're turning us out. They say they've already given us more time than they consider necessary for someone to agree to sell. Now the authority's using its powers and compelling us to sell."

Marisa turned pale. "All of us? Me, as well?"

"But of course, dear," Mrs. Worrell answered. "I own all six houses, don't I?"

"We're fighting it," Elwyn told her. "We have the right of appeal."

"I'm not giving in," Mrs. Worrell declared, "and that's flat. They'll have to carry me out of here feet first!"

"I've written the letter," Elwyn said, "I've got the draft copy here. You couldn't type it at work, could you? It might make it seem more official."

"Of course I will. I'm with you to the bitter end. Can't we demand a public inquiry?"

"That's exactly what I'm going to do."

Mrs. Worrell, still stunned, said, "I've got nowhere to go, nowhere. It's been my home for more years than I can remember. I could never get used to a new place at my time of life."

As soon as Marisa arrived at the office, she typed the letter making a formal objection to the compulsory purchase of the property. The letter also asked for a public inquiry. Jan came in. For once she was early, arriving before the other typists.

"Working already?" she asked. "You put me to shame."

Marisa told her what she was doing and Jan looked a little guilty. "I knew about it, dearie. Neville told me it was coming. I didn't like to say anything, but—"

"It's all right, Jan, I can't really blame you."

"I think you're wasting your time in appealing, Marisa. Everything's against you. Only two of the six houses are occupied, aren't they? And you must admit the houses are hardly works of art."

"All the same, it's been home to all of us for years, especially Mrs. Worrell. She'll be the one to feel it most."

"If you have to move out, where will you go?"

"I haven't the ghost of an idea. Become one of the legion of homeless, I suppose. Or find rooms." The prospect was bleak.

Jan said, "No chance of you and Dirk—?"

"None at all. He — he came to see me last night." Jan looked hopeful. "Of course, we quarrelled. I don't know what's happened to him. Almost every word he spoke he tried to hurt me."

Jan frowned. "Pity. But," she shrugged, "not all marriages work out. You simply married the wrong man, that's all."

"But I didn't, Jan!"

"My dear, if it's like that . . . I honestly thought you'd grown to hate him. I thought it was Elwyn—"

"Don't you start about Elwyn. I had enough from Dirk last night."

Jan looked hurt at her tone, and Marisa apologised again.

"It's all right, Marisa. I can guess how you feel. But isn't it going to be hell for you, seeing Dirk every day?"

"There's nothing I can do about it, is there?"

Jan gave her a warning frown, then changed it into a welcom-

25

ing smile. Someone was coming into the typists' room. Dirk stood beside Marisa. "Done those specifications yet?"

Jan looked from one to the other.

"How could I?" Marisa snapped. "I've only just arrived."

"But you're working. Aren't you?"

She covered the letter in the typewriter with her hand, but he merely caught her wrist and pulled her hand away. He read what she had typed. "You're wasting your time," he said, and walked out.

"Oh, dear," said Jan, frowning, and got on with her work.

Marisa typed the specifications and ran off the copies required on the duplicator. Then she took them to Dirk's office. He accepted them with a brief "Thanks."

"What did you mean," she challenged, "by saying I'm wasting my time? We're asking for a public inquiry."

"My dear girl," he leaned back in his chair, "the result is a foregone conclusion. You know the Council already owns the temporary car park site at the end of the garden?" She nodded. "Well, there's a private company, a property developer who is interested in buying it, but only if the land on which the houses stand goes with it. They've already offered a very large sum. If the Council can free the land adjacent to the car park – Mrs. Worrell's land – they'll sell to the developer and the money they get will help to reduce the rates. The developer will be granted the necessary planning permission quite quickly – in the circumstances that's almost a hundred per cent certain – and a block of offices will go up on the site. So you see, you're bound to lose. The houses are worthless. It's the land that's valuable."

"The houses may be worthless to you, but it's my home I'm fighting for. Where would I go if they pulled it down?"

"That," he said, flicking through the specifications, "is your problem."

"How can you be so unfeeling? It was your home once. Doesn't it hold any memories?"

"Plenty. Most of which I should like to forget."

With an effort she controlled her voice. "You say the nicest things!"

26

Dirk frowned, but did not look at her. "I do, don't I?"

Marisa went to the door.

His voice followed her. "And I'll tell you something else." She waited. "As soon as that land becomes available – as it will, whatever action you may choose to take – and planning permission is granted, there's a distinct possibility that this firm will be given the contract to design the building which will go up on the site, and as the senior architect I shall probably be given the job."

Unbelievingly she asked, "And you'd take it?"

"Like a shot."

She drew her breath. "You're nothing but a traitor!"

"Thanks," he said mildly.

"And I'll tell you this," her eyes blazed, "the Worrells and I are sticking together."

"I have no doubt of that."

"If the authorities want us out, they'll have to evict us – forcibly."

"I warn you – you might get hurt."

"I'll risk that."

Dirk looked pained. "Then you're an even bigger fool than I thought you were."

She flung out of the room.

Elwyn contacted the local newspaper. He considered it the best way to bring the public's attention to their plight. He told Marisa that the news editor had shown interest and was sending a reporter. "You don't object, do you?"

"Not at all," she answered. "But don't send him in to me, Elwyn. It would mean dragging Dirk's name into it, and that wouldn't really be fair."

"Dirk's hardly been fair to you, has he? Walking off and leaving you . . ."

She could not tell him that he had been the cause of Dirk's leaving her. He might become even more possessive if he knew that.

"All you need to do," she said, "is to make out a good case

27

for our being allowed to stay there. You could say how much it means to your mother to be left alone by the authorities, and so on."

He looked at his watch. "I'd better go. The reporter's due in ten minutes."

Dirk rang through to the typists' office first thing next morning and asked Marisa to go to him.

"He's early, isn't he?" Jan commented. "What does he want you for?"

"To dictate some letters, I suppose. Mr. Garner told him he could share me as secretary until he gets one of his own."

"Bit tactless of old Garner, wasn't it? Doesn't he know what's happened between you?"

"Of course, but," Marisa shrugged, "business is business. Personal matters shouldn't enter into it."

"All the same ... Incidentally, Neville says Dirk's got a furnished flat in a new block in the centre of the town."

"Thanks for telling me," Marisa said, determinedly noncommittal. "I didn't know."

She caught Jan's look of sympathy as she picked up her notebook and pencil.

Dirk said he only had one letter and would she please sit down. He dictated the letter and said, "Before you go, I want to tell you I've instructed the solicitor that I'm increasing the maintenance allowance I'm paying you."

"But why?" She knew she sounded ungracious.

"Why?" He doodled on his blotter, drawing a child's picture of a house. "Because now I've seen the appalling conditions you're living in, I realise that the amount we agreed on three years ago is not enough. I feel partly responsible because it was through your marriage to me that you got that house."

"There's no need for you to feel guilty about it. Whatever I did I did with my eyes open."

His head came up, his expression hard. "Yes, I'm sure you did. Wide open. And calculating."

"You do think a lot of me!" Her eyes moistened. "I don't know why you ever married me."

28

He smiled unpleasantly. "To be perfectly honest, nor do I. I think at the time I believed you'd make me a good and faithful wife. An error of judgment on my part, caused purely by youth and inexperience."

If he was going to be nasty, so could she. What did it matter that in the circumstances they had no right to be discussing their personal lives, that it was work they should be doing?

"And I thought," she blurted out, "that you would make me a good husband. How wrong I was!"

"At least we think alike on one point – that our marriage should never have taken place."

"Then let me go!"

"All in good time. You'll have to learn to be patient. So will Elwyn. He'll get you one day. But I warn you, I shall hold out until the last minute, until the law forces me to let you go." He contemplated her with a half-smile, as though a new line of thought had entered his mind. "I might even contest the divorce. It wouldn't stop the law granting it to you, but it would probably make things more difficult for you." He leaned back and watched her, his eyes half-closed. "Yes, I might even do that, if only to make Elwyn Worrell suffer the torments of jealousy I suffered in the past. I got over that long ago, of course, but it was hell while it lasted. Yes," his smile was sadistic now, "it would be good to see him endure the purgatory you inflicted on me. You know, I'm beginning to be glad I came back."

Marisa stood up. "I don't want your magnanimity, or your extra money. As far as I'm concerned, you can instruct the solicitor to stop the allowance altogether. I don't need it. I'm earning a reasonable salary."

"That I will not do. When you leave your present premises," she began to object, but he persisted, "as you will have to, however much you try to fool yourself you won't, you'll need the money I'm paying you. You'll need it for the higher rent you'll have to pay, and for the increase in your cost of living."

She knew there was nothing she could do about it. "Thank you." She dragged the words out ungraciously.

He nodded and dismissed her.

Elwyn got the publicity he wanted. On the front page of the local paper was a large picture of Elwyn and his mother. "Son fights for mother's right to live in peace", was the headline. "My mother," said Mr. Elwyn Worrell, "has lived in this house since the early days of her marriage many years ago. She's a widow now, and an invalid. It would kill her to have to move." Marisa thought that was putting it a little strongly, but knew he had said it for effect.

"It's not only us," the reporter alleged Elwyn had told him, "the other person affected is our tenant and neighbour, a young married woman living on her own, cruelly deserted by her husband. She'd have nowhere to go . . ."

Marisa flung the paper down. How could Elwyn have said that? He had promised not to mention Dirk. But of course, she supposed he hadn't. He had only mentioned him by implication, to draw attention to her plight, to gain sympathy and support. And the reporter really had piled on the agony.

She took off her coat and hung it in the hall cupboard then made herself some tea. Knowing Elwyn would be out that evening, she called on Mrs. Worrell to make sure she was comfortable and had everything she wanted.

Elwyn had banked up the fire before he left and Marisa found his mother in an armchair, gloating over the newspaper article. "They've put us on the front page, dear!" she exclaimed. "That'll make people sit up and take notice. They haven't got us out yet, have they? You see they've mentioned you?"

Marisa said gently, yes, she'd read the article, and hoped it would help their cause. She gave Mrs. Worrell some books to read, then left her, saying she had some ironing to do.

It was some time later that she heard the noise. She had finished the ironing and was in the kitchen when there was a terrifying crash, like glass breaking, from the front of the house. She raced up the steps and along the hallway and switched on the sitting-room light. A brick, which had been hurled into the room from the street, had smashed through the window and scattered glass all over the carpet. It was not until she bent down to pick up the brick that she saw the remains of the cut-glass vase which had stood on the windowsill. It had been a wedding present and she had valued it more than all her other possessions. Now only the base remained, its edges jagged and dangerous.

She heard children's voices in the distance and rushed to open the front door. They saw her and ran away, jeering as they went. There was nothing she could do. If she had shouted at them they would have drowned her words with laughter.

She went back to stare at the mess. The wind was driving through the gaping hole. It had started to rain and that was coming in, too. Marisa held her head. Something would have to be done to close that gap in the window pane. She couldn't go to bed and leave it like that.

Elwyn was out and she had no idea when he would be back. The first thing to be done, her dazed brain tried to tell her, was to clear up the mess. She got out the vacuum cleaner, but some of the particles of glass were too large to be sucked in. She bent down and with great care picked up the larger pieces and dropped them into the waste paper basket.

She held the remains of the vase on her palm. It seemed symbolic. Its end had been inevitable, she supposed. Like their marriage.

The key turned in the lock and Dirk filled the doorway. He saw her stunned expression, looked at the glass on the floor then at the window pane. Marisa pointed to the brick.

"Who threw that?" he asked.

"Children."

"Why?"

She shrugged. "That story in the paper, I suppose."

He didn't ask, what story? He picked his way across the littered carpet like someone stepping over an ice-covered pond. He took the remains of the vase from her hand.

She stared up at him, uncomprehending. "That's all that's left of it."

"Well? It was only a flower vase."

"It was one of our wedding presents."

"So what? It's gone now. You can't put it together again."

31

He paused. "Any more than you can put our marriage together again." He threw the broken vase away.

The wind whistled through the smashed window pane and as they turned to look, rain sprayed their faces. "That will have to be boarded up for a start," Dirk remarked.

"I know. But I don't know how."

"Couldn't you have asked beloved Elwyn?" Even now he had to be sarcastic.

"He's out."

"Good thing I came, then, isn't it?"

"Why did you come?"

"That will keep. Now, have you any pieces of wood, packing cases or even cardboard?"

"I don't know."

He smiled mockingly. "Helpless without a man, aren't you?"

"Try the cellar," she suggested. "You'll need a torch. The light doesn't work down there any more."

He tutted loudly. "Everything's going to rack and ruin. Where will I find a torch?"

"On my bedside table."

He sprinted up the stairs, found what he wanted and came down again. Marisa switched on the cleaner and began to clear up the mess. Dirk returned from the cellar with a large piece of board. His voice came loudly over the noise of the vacuum cleaner.

"My God, what a state this house is in! The sooner you're out of it the better."

She switched off the cleaner. "I don't see what concern it is of yours how I live."

"I still happen to be your husband," he said mildly, "however much the idea may upset you." He pulled a chair into position under the broken window. "Got a hammer? And nails? Or is that asking too much?"

"If I have, it's only what you left behind."

"Where? In the same place?"

She nodded.

"Nothing much has changed around here, has it?"

32

It did not take him long to hammer the board into place. "That should keep the weather out, even if it does make the house even more depressing."

She put the cleaner away. "Thanks for what you've done. Would you like some tea? Or coffee?"

"Coffee, if you're making some." He followed her into the kitchen and looked around. "A housewife's dream." He inspected the chipped sink, the wooden draining board, rough with protruding splinters. He passed the sole of his shoe over the uneven concrete floor. "And you'd defend this place to the last, with your life, if necessary?"

"It's the only home I've got," she muttered. "It may not be a palace, but it holds memories."

"And what memories!"

"Why did you come? To bait me?" She carried the coffee into the front room and handed him a cup. He took it and sat in the armchair opposite her, where he used to sit when the house was his home.

"To tell you I've found you somewhere to live."

"But I live here."

He ignored her statement. "I heard about it this evening and came straight away to tell you. There's a list of people wanting the flat, but the chap who told me about it – he's an estate agent – said he would hold it until tomorrow morning. It's two rooms and kitchen in a semi-detached house. The couple downstairs are elderly and want a steady, reliable tenant."

She knew she should thank him for his consideration, but said, "Then I'm surprised you thought of me."

He drank some coffee. "I'll let that remark pass, although the urge to throw it back in your beautiful face is overwhelming. Well, shall I tell the agent you'll take it?"

"No. But thank you for telling me about it."

Dirk clattered his cup back on to the saucer. "If you aren't the most stubborn misguided female I've come across! Turning down an excellent flat without giving it a moment's thought."

"I'm not leaving here. I'm fighting to the bitter end."

"And bitter it will be, let me tell you." He got up and walked

33

about restlessly. "You must be mad to think you can win against the authorities. Can't you see the inevitable when it's right in front of your eyes?"

"We've asked for a public inquiry."

"And on what grounds do you suppose you'll succeed? They'll send an official inspector round. One look at these rabbit holes will convince him they're better knocked down than left standing."

He saw the local newspaper lying on the floor beside her chair. He picked it up and she knew he could not avoid seeing the photograph of Elwyn and his mother and the article about them.

The derision in his eyes turned into anger. He read aloud, " 'Cruelly deserted by her husband'?" He stared at her. "*Deserted?* You know damned well it was not desertion. We agreed to separate. We even signed a document to that effect."

"I know, but I didn't see the reporter. Those are Elwyn's words, not mine."

He flung down the paper. "One of these days I'll give that interfering devil just what he's asking for! It would give me indescribable pleasure to put him in his place once and for all. I should have done it years ago."

"Why don't you divorce me?" she cried. "Then I'd be off your conscience and you wouldn't have to worry about me or Elwyn ever again."

"Divorce you? So that you can marry that crass idiot? Make everything easy and straightforward for you? Not on your life!"

He walked across the room, then stood quite still in front of her. A brooding malicious look crept into his eyes. "I'll make a bargain with you. A condition. If you fulfil it, I'll give you the divorce you want."

Her heart beat painfully fast as his regard changed into anticipation and he looked her over. "What condition?" she asked faintly.

"If you give me what every husband has a right – a legal right – to expect from his wife. Once. Just once more."

34

Marisa faced him, scarlet with anger. "How could you ask it? It would be an empty, meaningless act."

He moved to the door and his smile taunted her. "Nevertheless it would be your way out, your only way out for a long time to come. Just think about it, will you?"

He left the house and seconds later his car roared down the road.

CHAPTER III

WHEN Marisa told Elwyn next morning about the brick coming through the window, he asked, "How did you manage to board it up on your own?"

"Dirk called when I was trying to clear up the mess. He found the board in the cellar and did the job."

"Dirk? What was he doing here?"

She told him why Dirk had come. "But I turned his offer down. I'm staying here."

"I should think so. We're sticking together over this, all three of us."

Once again she found herself resenting his attitude, as though he had more right to her than Dirk. But she answered, "Don't worry, I won't let you or your mother down. Not after all her kindness to me in the past."

He looked satisfied and waved her off to work.

At lunchtime a large section of the office staff patronised a nearby restaurant. The men, including Neville, would push two or three tables together – the management, being used to them, were long-suffering – and talk shop. Jan would sit as near to her husband as she could, and Marisa would share her table.

One lunchtime they were watching the men as they waited for their lunches to be served. Dirk was with them and as usual he seemed to be dominating the discussion. He took out a pencil and started to sketch the plan of a building on the plastic-covered table-top. Others added details to his drawing or took out envelopes and old letters from their pockets and drew on them.

"It's a good thing," Jan commented, "the management here are easy-going. Do you know, I've seen them having to use scouring powder to get those pen and pencil marks off?"

Marisa laughed. Despite her circumstances, she felt happy. Dirk's presence brought unusual animation to her habitually sad face and she had caught his puzzled eyes upon her once or twice. "I've even known them use the menu cards. What other customers must think when they see the hieroglyphics those men leave behind, I don't know."

When lunch was over, Neville strolled across to his wife and Jan, excusing herself, went out with him. A little embarrassed at being left alone, Marisa picked up her bag and pulled on her coat.

She did not notice Dirk walking over to her table. "Going already?" She jumped at the sound of his voice. "Sorry to startle you. Sit down for a few minutes, will you?"

The other men looked at them curiously and drifted away, paying their bills as they went.

Dirk signalled to the waitress to bring two coffees.

"I've finished my lunch," Marisa said, resenting his autocratic action.

"I know. Another coffee won't hurt you."

The coffees were put in front of them and he offered Marisa the sugar. "Did I hear you say the other evening that you were producing a play?"

"Yes." She wondered why he could possibly be interested in that.

"And your good friend Elwyn Worrell is in it?"

"Yes." She was on the defensive at once. "What of it?"

"Just wondered. It's not really relevant." He stirred his coffee. "In the past three years, having had little better to occupy my mind in my leisure hours, I've become interested in the theatre, via amateur dramatics."

Marisa commented, holding back the hope that was tugging at her like a dog straining to get at another, "I have heard that an interest in the theatre isn't unusual among architects."

"That's quite true. It appeals to the artistic side of their nature. But speaking for myself, I like dabbling in visual experiments, making something seem larger or smaller than it really is by using perspective. You know, constructing things like couches or beds to a scale much smaller than they are in reality, but doing it so subtly that the audience doesn't realise it. And I find the de-

37

sign problems that crop up a challenge to my ingenuity. Anyway," he smiled at her for the first time, and her body felt bathed in warmth as though someone had switched on the sun for a few seconds, "I was going to ask you, as producer, whether you could use my services as a stage designer. As I said, I've had some experience. I've got good references." She hesitated, overwhelmed by his offer. "Have I sold myself well enough to get the job?"

She fenced, not wishing to sound too eager. "You don't know what the play is about. It might prove too difficult for you to tackle."

Dirk stated positively, "Nothing is too difficult for me to tackle. The more demanding a project on my resources the more I rise to it." He added cryptically, and with emphasis, "And I don't only mean architectural or theatrical design. Well, what's the answer?"

"Yes, thanks, if you want to come in with us. We're all very amateur, but we enjoy it and we hope the audiences do, too. You would certainly give the production more polish."

"Thanks. That's a compliment. I've never known you praise my work before."

She coloured. "I've always thought highly of you – as an architect."

"As an architect," he echoed flatly. "But not – definitely not – as a husband."

The violence and bitterness of their last quarrel sounded again in her ears as if she were listening to the repeat of a particularly unhappy radio play. "You walked out on me."

"And you know why." He pushed back his chair and took her lunch bill from the table as well as that for the coffee. She tried to take it from him.

"That's mine."

"Let me have the pleasure." He added sarcastically, "Since I'm going to work on this production under your direction, we've at least got to appear to be friendly."

Outside in the street he asked, "When's the next rehearsal?"

"Tonight. Can you make it?"

38

"I think so. What time and where?"

She told him and he left her, saying he had a meeting to attend.

Mr. Garner was out and Mr. Hilsby called Marisa in to take dictation. He dealt with half a dozen letters and then he sighed.

"Do you know what I'm going to do soon, my dear? I'm taking my wife and myself off on a long winter holiday. I'm going to find the sunshine. And then, do you know what? I think I'll retire."

"But surely you're not old enough, Mr. Hilsby?"

"Now that's a nice compliment. I left sixty behind a year or so ago, you know. My wife wants me to retire, and to tell you the truth, I'm feeling the strain. I simply can't keep up with it." He looked at her. "You should know how necessary it is for an architect to keep up with the times. You're married to one, aren't you?"

She wondered if that was a leading question, to discover how things stood between herself and Dirk. "I – was. Our marriage has broken down."

"He's back here, isn't he? You'll come together again, I'm convinced of that."

"I'm afraid that's impossible. Our marriage simply didn't work."

"Perhaps you never gave it a chance," he said gently, "perhaps you didn't understand the sort of life an architect has to lead. They're not tied down to office hours, you know. I've known them work on a project sometimes until well into the night. A wife has to learn to tolerate it. Perhaps you were too young to understand?"

She frowned again, remembering her resentment of the way Dirk never seemed to stop working.

"Perhaps."

"And another thing. They have to lead lives which give them the opportunity to meet people – mix socially with possible clients, for instance, show a keen interest in local affairs and so on. And the higher an architect climbs in his profession, the

39

greater the demands on his spare time. The more ability he has the more he advances and the more he has to give out to his work. Now take your husband."

"Your husband", he kept saying. Part of her delighted in the expression, but part of her rejected it. Dirk was not really her husband any more.

"He has ability," Mr. Hilsby persisted. "No doubt about it. When I go, you know he'll be offered my position, and that it will mean a considerable increase in status and responsibility for him?"

Marisa looked down at her notebook. "Yes, I did know."

"He's young. He has ideas, he can face the future, unlike me. Somehow I simply cannot accept the way architecture is going. Take present trends, for example. Architecture nowadays is as near rock bottom as it can go. It hasn't any frills or flourishes. Its lines are classic, plain. Some call it beautiful, but to me, it's not. And architecture of the future!" He sounded appalled and shook his head. "As I said, it's time I got out. I'm a traditionalist to the core. I'm taking a long holiday. It will give me time to think things over." He looked at his watch. "I mustn't keep you, must I? You're a good listener, Mrs. Sterling!" He laughed. "I'll have to tell your husband that. I must get working on that man of yours. Can't have you two young people going on like this!"

She wanted to say, "Thank you, but you'd be wasting your time. There's as much chance of our coming together again as there is of the Arctic and Antarctic meeting at the Equator!"

Instead she smiled and left him.

Someone had put on a record and the hall, cheerless, chilly, its high, uncurtained windows slashed by rain, was filled with the poignant beauty of *Greensleeves*.

Marisa, untying her rainhood and removing her coat, preceded Elwyn into the hall and saw Dirk standing alone beside the record player, hands in pockets, lost in thought. As she ran the comb through her hair, she listened. The melancholy of the music plunged her into the past when, early in their marriage,

40

she and Dirk had sat, arms entwined, listening to it. They had bought a second-hand copy of the record one afternoon in the local market. The record player had been second-hand, too. Most of their possessions had been someone else's cast-offs. Now their marriage had gone the same way.

Dirk looked up, eyes unguarded and expectant, and saw her. Then he saw Elwyn by her side and his expression hardened, like liquid concrete solidifying. The music came to an end, the spell was broken, the present was thrust upon them both like an impenetrable mist across the past.

The others, standing round the hall in groups, came to life. The producer had arrived, the person they had been waiting for, the cohesive factor which united them and gave them meaning. They threw off the inertia imposed on them by the dreary surroundings and greeted her cheerfully.

Elwyn took Marisa's coat and shook from it the slight spattering of rain it had acquired on the short journey from the car to the hall. The elaborate care with which he handled it was due partly to the professional respect for clothes imposed on him by his work, and partly to his desire to impress with his attentiveness the man watching them so narrowly from the other end of the hall. The manner in which he placed Marisa's coat side by side with his acquired a certain symbolism. These two belong together, the action said, just as their owners do.

Dirk, however, seemed singularly unimpressed. He gave a passing smile, and for the few seconds it survived, it was cynical.

Marisa performed the introductions. "Come on, everyone, and meet Dirk." He had moved to join the group. "He's very kindly offered to supervise the scenic side of the production."

"Ah, we've acquired what is technically known as an artistic director," one of the young men murmured.

Marisa said to Dirk, "This is Elwyn Worrell, our leading man."

"Hallo, Dirk," murmured Elwyn, his smile ingratiating. His extreme annoyance when Marisa had told him Dirk would be at the rehearsal had gone into hiding. "He's offered to help with the

41

scenery," Marisa had said in the car. "His efforts will be much more professional than we've ever had before."

But Elwyn still hadn't liked the idea.

Now Dirk looked at Elwyn and said dryly, "We have met before."

Marisa went round the group. "Patty, in charge of make-up." Dirk smiled and nodded. "Norman's our electrician and he's usually worked on the scenery, too."

"Be glad of help," Norman murmured.

"Matt, stage manager, Anna's in charge of costumes, and here's Philip, Judi, Tom –"

"Ham actors," said Tom.

"Don't forget me," said Sally, her eyes on Dirk.

"Our leading lady," Marisa said, "Sally Barnes."

Sally sauntered across to Dirk, presenting herself for his inspection. "Good to see a new male around here."

Dirk's appraising eyes seemed to appreciate the charms of the leading lady, too. She was short, which enabled her to gaze with a slightly helpless air into men's faces. Her figure tended to plumpness but was shapely. Her eyes were bright, as though a light had been perpetually left switched on.

"Dirk what?" she asked.

With barely discernible hesitation he told her, "Sterling."

"Sterling?" She turned to Marisa. "Another Sterling? That's odd. Any –?"

"No," Dirk broke in, with a quick, sly smile at Marisa, "no connection at all."

"We – we work in the same office," Marisa said, feeling a thrust of pain at his swift disavowal of any relationship to her.

"Of course," said Sally to Marisa, "your name's spelt with an 'e', isn't it?" She looked at Dirk. "Yours has got an 'i' in it, I expect."

Dirk did not answer. Elwyn stayed silent, too, as Marisa knew he would.

Dirk gave Sally an encouraging smile. She responded by touching his arm. "I wish you were the leading man," she said.

He laughed. "Having met the leading lady, so do I."

42

The others laughed, too. Marisa turned away sharply. "Everyone got copies of the play?"

"I haven't," said Dirk.

"Share mine," said Sally. She pressed close against him and held her book in front of him.

"He can't," snapped Marisa. "You'll be on the stage. He'll be down here watching. Until we get another copy, he'll have to share mine."

"Pity." Dirk lifted an arm and squeezed Sally's shoulder. He looked maliciously at Marisa, who had made her face blank, but could not hide the pain in her eyes. Then he moved to stand beside her.

"On stage, everyone," Marisa called. Elwyn went with the others.

Dirk whispered in her ear, "Sorry you accepted my offer of help?"

"You can have as many girl-friends as you like," she whispered back fiercely.

"Thanks for your permission," he replied blandly, "but I don't need it any more."

"Let's change the subject," she muttered, "and get down to business."

He smiled and looked over her shoulder at the script.

"Last time," she called to the cast, who were standing about on the stage, "we went through the words. Tonight we'll run through the movements."

Dirk found a chair and sat beside Marisa. To her relief they were joined by the others who were involved in the production side, which meant that she and Dirk would for the moment have to pretend they were friends. Dirk put his fingers round her wrist and moved the hand that was holding the book so that it was between them, instead of on her lap, and rested his arm along the back of her chair. Their faces were so near her hair brushed his cheek and with his fingers he pushed it away, tucking it behind her ear. They might have been on intimate terms.

Elwyn, from his raised postion on the stage, watched every movement between them, as Dirk must have known he would.

43

The cast, unaccustomed to their roles, were unrelaxed and wooden. Reading instead of speaking the words, their voices were expressionless.

Marisa sighed. "You'll have to loosen up," she said. "This is a satirical comedy, not a tragedy. Of course, we can't do much until you all know your words. Let's have the scene between Courtenay and Alys, where Courtenay's trying to persuade Alys to leave her fiancé and go away with him."

Elwyn and Sally took their places alone on the stage and went through their lines. Marisa put a hand to her head. "That's no good, Elwyn, you'll have to be much more forceful. You've got to be domineering, not gently persuasive. No girl would ever listen to you if you spoke to her like that, let alone run away with you!"

"Pretend it's Marisa you're talking to," Dirk called out, and everyone, except Elwyn, laughed.

Elwyn's pale cheeks were stained with scarlet at the subtle taunt. The others thought it was with embarrassment. Only Marisa and Dirk knew it was with anger. Marisa flashed a look at Dirk which should have blinded him, but he didn't even blink. He merely deflected it with a grin.

Dirk's taunt, however, had had some effect, because Elwyn's performance grew more spirited, although still strictly within the bounds imposed by his personality. Marisa knew there was a limit to his ability for dramatic self-expression, but she also knew that for this particular part he would have to be coaxed into breaking through that limit. Sally, Marisa hoped and believed, was a good enough actress to make him do it.

When the rehearsal was over, the cast and helpers drifted home. Elwyn found Marisa's coat.

"Can I give you a lift?" Dirk asked Marisa.

"Thanks, but Elwyn brought me. He's taking me home." Elwyn smiled, a gloating, self-satisfied smile, and helped Marisa on with her coat.

Dirk shrugged. "I've done my duty. I've offered my estranged wife a lift." His eyes roamed round the hall, now emptying fast.

"That leaves you free to take Sally home," Marisa said frigidly.

Dirk smiled mockingly. "How well you can read my mind, darling. An ability acquired as a result of our intimacy in the past, no doubt." He watched for the effect of his remark on Marisa's companion, and was not disappointed.

"Sally?" he called across the hall. "Want a lift?"

"Love one," she answered, joining him.

Without another word he took her arm and led her towards the door.

First thing next morning Marisa called in to see Mrs. Worrell.

Elwyn opened the door. "Mother's excited. Come upstairs and see her. We've had a letter."

Mrs. Worrell's pain-worn face was flushed, her hand shaking as she held out the letter. "Read it, dear. There's going to be a public inquiry."

"They want us to send them a list of our objections to the compulsory purchase," Elwyn said. "We're advising a solicitor."

"It says," Marisa commented, "you can send witnesses to the inquiry. Will you go?"

"Of course."

"And me, Elwyn," said his mother.

"I don't know that you should. It'll be a strain for you, sitting through that."

"But, Elwyn, if they see the state I'm in, and that I can hardly put one foot in front of the other sometimes, you never know, it might touch their hearts." To Marisa, "Don't you agree, dear?"

"It might well do, Mrs. Worrell." Marisa said to Elwyn, feeling a little like a traitor, "You won't want me to appear as a witness, will you? After all, I'm just a tenant . . ."

He took it quite well. "Not if you don't want to. The solicitor acting for us would probably put your case better than you could yourself."

She smiled at him in her gratitude and she might have given him a costly present. He put his arm round her. His mother regarded them with a satisfied smile. "We'll stick together, won't we, the three of us? We'll fight to the bitter end."

Marisa drove to work and parked in the usual place. She

gathered her belongings and got out as another car swung into the space beside hers.

"Well," said Dirk, getting out, "if it isn't the producer herself." He looked her car over. "Second-hand?"

"Of course. Where would I get the money from to buy a new one?"

He shrugged. "Your worthy neighbour and boy-friend, perhaps? After all, it's not unknown for men to give their women presents."

They walked across the road to the office. "Must you start first thing in the morning?" she snapped. "He's not my man and I'm not his woman. Is that clear?"

He looked down at her and raised an eyebrow. "Not really. After all, he was behaving last night as though you were his to command."

The idea of Elwyn commanding anything or anyone made Marisa want to laugh aloud. "If that's what you think, then think on," she said loftily, and walked in the opposite direction, making for the typists' office.

She greeted the other girls with a forced smile. Marcia, who sat across the room, seemed to want to talk, but after a few words, Marisa brought the conversation to an end by starting work.

Mr. Garner called her in and he soon dealt with his mail. When she returned to her desk Jan said, "Your husband sent for you." Involuntarily she winced at the term. "What's the matter? He is still your husband, isn't he?"

Marisa laughed uncomfortably. "Yes, but – well, I suppose I haven't really got used to having him back here. It's not as though we're –" She stopped.

"I know, living together. All the same, he sent for you, so you'd better go, hadn't you?"

Dirk gave a provocative smile as she went in, leaned back in his seat as though it were a luxuriously upholstered armchair and linked his hands behind his head. "It's so nice having you at my beck and call. And to know that whatever orders I give you you have to carry out without argument." He looked at her narrowly, sadistically. "If I were to tell you to go out and buy an expensive box of chocolates for me to give to my girl-friend, you'd have to do it, wouldn't you?"

"You haven't got a girl-friend!"

"Haven't I? How do you know? He leaned on the desk. "Sally's a – nice girl, isn't she?"

Marisa examined her pencil which was waiting, poised, to take dictation. "Is she? I wouldn't know. I only know her as a tolerably good amateur actress."

"Ah, then obviously I'm better acquainted with her than you are. After all, I took her home last night."

She stood up. "Is that all you wanted to say? Because if so, will you excuse me? I have work to do."

"No, I will not excuse you." He became businesslike and sorted through some papers. "I have a conference coming along in a month or two in the Midlands. The subject deals with new trends in architecture. It's being run by a regional advisory council of which I'm the secretary. I've written a paper which I shall be reading to the conference and I should like it typed." He handed it to her. "I shall want to take a secretary with me because I'll need a detailed transcript of the proceedings, as I shall have to make a full report to the committee."

"You're not –" she faltered, "you're not asking me to go with you?"

"Of course not, for obvious reasons."

"Jan won't want to go because of Neville."

"I realise that. It will have to be one of the other girls."

"There's Marcia, Angela ..."

"Are they attached? Have they got husbands?"

"No. Not even engaged as far as I know."

"All right, I'll have to make enquiries. The point is that I must book a room for myself and one for whoever I take with me."

"Is that all?"

"Yes, thanks."

She looked at the pages of handwritten notes he had given her. "This may take me some time. I have Mr. Garner's work to do."

"No great hurry. Do it when you can." Dirk grinned. "You see, I'm not a slave-driver."

"It's just as well," she answered with a smile. "Because I'm no one's slave."

"You win that one, Mrs. Sterling," he said.

Leonard Hilsby went away for his long winter holiday. It was rumoured that he might not return to work and that his retirement was imminent. This speculation was reinforced by the fact that Dirk Sterling moved into Mr. Hilsby's office.

Marisa assumed that Dirk was now officially Harris Garner's partner. She wondered if the name of the firm would be altered from Hilsby, Garner to Garner, Sterling and Associates.

She also wondered if Dirk would still want to take part in the production of the play. Apparently he did. He had attended another rehearsal and had had a long discussion with Norman Smith, the electrician in the group.

One morning Marisa went to Dirk's new office. It was strange seeing him sitting at Mr. Hilsby's desk. Somehow she missed the older man's warmth and understanding. When she had gone in to see Mr. Hilsby, her heart had certainly not thumped as it was doing now.

She held out a copy of the play. "It came by post this morning."

"Good." He took it from her. "Now I can really get down to work on it. Perhaps we could have a discussion some time about the backgrounds, to see if my ideas coincide with yours."

"There's a rehearsal tonight."

"I know, but unfortunately I'm tied up."

"Oh." She tried not to show her disappointment.

He flicked through the pages. "I'm having dinner with a client. A woman, a widow who wants a house built. I met her recently at an official function I attended and she asked me if I would tackle the planning of it privately." He looked up at her. "Nothing to do with the firm."

Marisa had to say something. "If she's a widow, why does she want a house built?"

48

"That's a question I never ask. It's my job to do the designing, not to ask questions."

She felt he had put her in her place.

"She's a rich widow. Her husband left her a lot of money. She has a young child, a son about six."

"So she's quite young herself?"

"Quite young. About my age."

"And you're having dinner with her?"

"I'm having dinner with her."

She wished he would stop echoing her words.

"Tonight." Dirk was smiling. He said softly, "We are legally separated, you know. I don't have to report all my movements and my motives to you."

She left his room and banged the door. Then she wished she hadn't, because in doing so she had given away to him how vulnerable she still was where he was concerned.

The public inquiry took place. The solicitor had put the case for the Worrells and Elwyn and his mother appeared as witnesses. They stated their objections and appealed for the compulsory purchase order to be rescinded and the houses left alone.

The appeal failed. The government inspector appointed to conduct the inquiry said he was sorry, but he could find no grounds on which to support the objectors' appeal, and would have to recommend that the local authority's powers of compulsory purchase be upheld.

He said the Government Minister to whom he was responsible would have the last word, but he felt convinced that when the Minister heard all the facts of the case, he would support the decision.

When Marisa called in to see Elwyn after work, she found his mother in tears. "I'm not giving in," she said, wiping her eyes. "I'm staying. Even if they send the bailiffs, I'm not budging. It's my home. I've nowhere else to go. It isn't even as if I was fit."

Marisa tried to comfort her, but it was a useless task. There was really no comfort to give. She told her, "I'll stick by you, Mrs. Worrell. I'll never forget how good you've been to me."

Mrs. Worrell said it was nothing, and she was like a daughter to her anyway.

Next morning Marisa told Jan, who told Neville, and Neville told Dirk. At lunchtime he sat beside her. Tactfully Jan joined Neville and the others.

"So you've lost your appeal?"

"It seems like it." She added, with defiance, "We're not giving in. We're staying put."

"They'll send the bailiffs, you realise that?" She nodded. "And they're not known for their gentleness in dealing with people who defy them. I'd hate you to get hurt."

"That," she muttered, "is either the biggest lie, or the biggest irony of the year."

He shrugged, pushing aside his empty coffee cup. "Where will you go?"

"I've no idea."

"Move in with Elwyn and his mother again?"

"No. In any case, they're not sure what they're going to do. Mrs. Worrell has a sister who could take her in temporarily."

"And Elwyn?" She shrugged. "You and he could always team up." Marisa looked at him to see if he was serious and found him smiling.

"His mother will get a lot of compensation from the local authority. They won't take the property into consideration – it's too tumbledown for that – but the land those houses stand on must be worth quite a bit by now. So it's in your interests to keep in with him, isn't it?" He was still smiling. "After all, when you marry him, you'll be marrying money, won't you, because he's the only heir to his mother's fortune."

There he was, her husband, sitting so close their arms were touching, and he was calmly discussing her marriage to another man.

"You're talking nonsense. I can't commit bigamy –"

"One day I'll let you go. When it suits me."

She was twisting her glass of water round so fast some of the contents spilt. "When we divorce each other I'm not marrying again. In any case, I'd never marry a man I didn't love."

50

"Now you're talking nonsense. You did it once, so —"

She turned on him fiercely, a denial on her lips, when Neville said behind them, "Having fun, you two?"

"Making it up?" Jan asked hopefully.

Dirk stood. "As a matter of fact, Neville, we were talking about what we're going to do when we get divorced."

Jan looked disappointed and as a kind of reflex action slipped her arm through her husband's and clung to him.

The Government Minister concerned duly ratified the decision of the inspector in charge of the public inquiry. The Worrells had finally lost and they and their tenant were given official notice to quit. Until it was there in her hand, Marisa had refused to believe it would happen. Now she knew that before long, despite the fact that they had decided to stay put until they were physically evicted, she would be one of the country's homeless.

Elwyn told her to pack her clothes in case of emergencies, but to leave everything else as it was. When the bailiffs came, he would help her to barricade the doors with some of the furniture.

Marisa told Jan what they intended to do and Jan tried without success to make her change her mind. That night after her meal, she wandered round the house. It was old and ugly, but she loved every bit of it. She had been happy there in the early days of her marriage. She had been miserable, too, but now the place was part of her. She looked at the wallpaper she and Dirk had chosen together, and dirty and torn though it was, she still loved it.

There was the room they had said their baby would sleep in — when they could afford to have one. There were the curtains she had spoilt when making them, and she had cried over. Dirk had comforted her. "We won't bother with curtains," he'd said, holding her in his arms and kissing her. "We'll do what our ancestors did, go to bed when it gets dark."

She wandered into the bedroom and lay down on the bed. It was here they had made love, and she remembered their joy in each other, the way they had clung to each other and kissed.

There was the key in the lock just as she had heard it in the past. It came to her with a shock that it was not her imagination. The front door had really opened and closed. She got up and went on to the landing. Dirk was looking up at her, and she realised that her hair must be untidy and her face stained with tears.

"What do you want?" she asked, hoping her belligerence would send him away before he saw how upset she was.

"Don't make your delight in my appearance so obvious," was all he said.

Marisa returned to the bedroom and combed her hair, hoping some powder would cover the blemishes her tears had produced. Then she went downstairs.

"What have you come for?"

"I heard from Jan that you intend to defy the notice to quit. I've come to try to persuade you to see reason."

"You're wasting your time. I'm sticking it out, together with the Worrells."

"All right, then you'll just have to take what's coming to you. Don't expect me to come to your rescue."

"I don't expect anything of you, not after the way you walked out on me." She turned away sharply, unable to keep the tears from her voice.

Dirk came up behind her, put his hands round her arms. "Marisa," he said softly, but she could not stand the touch of him because of the emotions it aroused, so she twisted away.

"My God," he said, his voice hard, "if you can't even bear the touch of my hands –" He wandered round the room.

"What are you doing?"

"If there's anything of mine here, I'm taking it."

Her temper snapped. "Take the lot!" she shouted. "Take the armchairs, the sideboard, the carpet, such as it is. Take the cutlery, the crockery, everything. You can have it now. I don't want it. I don't want anything I used to share with you . . . " She threw herself on to an armchair, buried her face in a cushion and sobbed.

52

He ignored her, going round the room looking in drawers, taking things now and then and putting them in his pockets. He went into the kitchen, the bedrooms, searching systematically in all the cupboards.

"These records," he said, coming in, "do you want them?" She did not answer. He put them in a carrier bag he had found and went away.

CHAPTER IV

DIRK did not attend many rehearsals at first. He said there was little point in his doing so at that stage. In any case, he was busy in his spare time working on the house he was designing.

What he did not say, but Marisa suspected, was that he was seeing a lot of his client. She had seen him driving about with her in his car, with her small son in the back seat. Once she had seen him driving the woman's car. When they were out together, they looked like a family.

"I wonder if she knows," Marisa thought miserably, "that she's running around with a married man." She looked the sort of woman, who, if she wanted anything enough, would let nothing stand in her way.

Once Dirk took his client to lunch at the restaurant they all patronised. She was blonde, her slim figure was wrapped in a fur coat which must have cost a fortune. Marisa envied her the poise and self-assurance which was obviously the by-product of the wealth she had inherited. Her son, almost too well-behaved for a child of his age, was with her. To Marisa's unhappy eyes, Dirk looked as if he were already the child's stepfather.

He introduced the woman to the others as "Luella Ackland, my client." He did not bother to take her across to meet Marisa.

One afternoon, Marisa returned from taking dictation from Mr. Garner when Jan said, agitatedly, "Elwyn phoned. He said the bailiffs have been at your house. They climbed in through a window and have put your things out on the front lawn."

"No!" Marisa sat down, feeling faint. She looked outside at the darkening afternoon. It was pouring with rain. "Oh, Jan, what can I do? I'll have to go home."

Home, had she said? She had no home now. And they had planned to barricade themselves in! She should have known that this was how the authorities would do it. When she told Mr. Garner, he was sympathetic and said she could go straight away.

Jan said, "If there's anything Neville and I can do to help –?"

"Thanks, Jan. If there is I'll let you know."

The sight that greeted Marisa as she got out of her car was like an appalling nightmare. She could not accept that it was really happening – and happening to her. She grew confused, like someone who had been knocked partially unconscious and was fighting the nausea and bewilderment that followed. Her eyes, clearing, saw, but her mind did not take in, that all her personal belongings, her furniture, suitcases, curtains, books, crockery – some of which was broken – were strewn about the front garden where they had been dumped by the bailiffs.

A group of people, umbrellas held high, were watching, and one of them said, with sympathy, "They yours, love?"

Marisa nodded, her eyes still not quite comprehending.

"What're you going to do, love? Got anywhere to go?"

Marisa tried to pull herself together. "No."

Elwyn came out, his face paler than usual, his eyes intense with anxiety. "I couldn't do a thing, Marisa. By the time my mother had struggled to the phone to warn me, they'd ransacked your house. They left ours out of respect for my mother. She begged them to wait until I came home. I called a taxi and they've taken her to her sister's across the town. Now I've promised the bailiffs I'll get packed up and go quietly. Luckily some of it's been done, in case of emergencies." He saw her distress and said helplessly, "I'm sorry it's come to this, Marisa. We meant to stay and fight, but –"

She started crying, she couldn't help it, and he put his arm round her awkwardly. "You're getting wet from the rain. Come into the dry." He led her into his house and she sobbed against him.

"We've got to do something about your things, Marisa." His voice was anxious. "We can't bring them in here. If they're left out there much longer, everything will be ruined."

She sobbed, still hiding her face against his chest like a defenceless child, "I don't know what to do .."

"Marisa?" It was Dirk's curt voice at the front door. "If you could tear yourself away from your beloved for a moment ... I need his help."

She lifted her head and Elwyn took his arms away. He seemed embarrassed. "Elwyn," Dirk said, "if you wouldn't mind giving me a hand with this tarpaulin? I've borrowed it from a builder I know. At least it should give some protection to those things out there, until they're otherwise disposed of."

Elwyn sat Marisa down in a chair which had been put in the hall for his mother and went outside with Dirk. It did not take them long to gather her belongings into a large pile and fix the tarpaulin into place.

Dirk reappeared. "Marisa, I've booked you a room at the Carlton." It was one of the largest hotels in the town. "You can spend a week or so there, while you work out what to do."

She said dully, "I can't afford the Carlton." She knew she should have thanked him, but she was beyond feeling grateful to anyone.

He ignored her statement and said to Elwyn, "You, I take it, have somewhere to go?"

"Yes, my aunt's. I'll join my mother there later."

Dirk looked round. "You've plenty to keep you occupied packing this stuff."

Marisa roused herself. "I'll stay and help Elwyn."

Dirk said quietly, "You are going to that hotel. You have enough on your plate without trying to get someone else out of trouble."

"But I can't leave Elwyn –"

"You go, Marisa," Elwyn urged. "I'll manage somehow. They've given me a couple of days."

Dirk asked her abruptly, "Got your car? Feel capable of driving it? Right, here are three cases and a holdall I found on the lawn. I take it they contain your clothes? The cases are wet, but I imagine the contents are reasonably dry. I've explained the position to the hotel management. They were sympathetic and I'm sure they'll help you if necessary."

He carried the cases to her car and drove off in his own in the opposite direction. The comfort of the hotel was a luxury she had never known before. She was welcomed sympathetically by the girl at the reception desk. "You're the lady we've been expecting. Been turned out of your house, haven't you? Your husband contacted us. Bad luck, especially on a day like this. Your husband said he would be joining you later." She gave Marisa the key to her room.

Joining her later? What did that mean? As Marisa followed the porter to the first floor, she was sure the girl had given her the wrong message. But the higher she climbed up the stairs, the more her fears mounted.

The porter left her as she fumbled with the key, trying to unlock the door of her room, she remembered the "condition" Dirk had imposed as her means of escape from their marriage. Surely he did not intend to impose that condition now? Having manoeuvred her into a situation from which she could not escape, to make such demands on her could only be construed as cruelty . . .

She opened the door and froze with dismay. It was not just a bedroom. There was a private bathroom attached. They must have made a mistake. She couldn't afford a room with a bath in a first-class hotel. But she knew that a mistake had not been made. This must be the apartment Dirk had booked for her. Perhaps it was all they had to offer tonight. Perhaps tomorrow she could ask them to move her to a more modest room.

She carried her cases in, closed the door and switched on the light. To her relief she saw that the room contained a single bed. She sank down on it, holding her head in her hands. Her mind was still reeling, she had not yet fully recovered her senses. In the darkness created by her hands, she told herself it had not happened, she wasn't really homeless. Soon she would go back to the house, find it as it had always been, there to welcome her.

She uncovered her eyes and reality stared her in the face like an enraged bull threatening to gore her. For the third time in her life her world had been felled like a tree in its prime. First there had been her mother's death and her father's remarriage. Then her husband had left her. Now had come the ultimate deprivation – eviction from the house that had been her home

Marisa sighed, trying to draw comfort from her present surroundings as a baby takes in milk from a bottle. Given time, she supposed, she would recover from this blow as she had recovered from all the others. Her natural resilience would see her through.

The clothes inside the cases seemed dry enough, but she did not unpack them. It was not worth it because she would not be in that particular bedroom long enough. Tomorrow she would move to another.

Dinner, according to the notice on the wall, was served from seven o'clock onwards, but she decided not to bother. No doubt if she rang reception she would be served with something light to eat in her room.

Her body felt stiff and soiled. A bath – she might as well make use of it while she still had it – would wash away the fatigue from her limbs. She wished it could wash the depression from her mind.

The abundant hot water acted as a palliative, blurring the edges of reality, softening it into a form her mind could begin, slowly, to accept. The water dripped from her as she climbed out on to the bathmat, and she coiled the soft white towel under her armpits and round her body.

The door opened and Dirk stood there. Marisa choked, "How did you get in?"

"On my own two feet, how else?" He leaned languidly against the wall and looked her over. "Do you make a habit of leaving all your doors unlocked? Perhaps you were expecting Elwyn?" He wandered across to the bathroom stool and sat on it, leaning back against the wall. "Well, go on, dry yourself. Why so coy? I've seen you in the bath – and out of it – before."

She tried being belligerent, but in her present situation it was hardly an effective emotion. "You've no right in here!"

"That I don't accept. I have every right in here."

He stood lazily and walked across to her. He ran his hands over her contours, saying softly, "I'd forgotten how beautiful you are." His hands, resting on her hips, impelled her towards him.

"As you said yourself," she cursed her voice for sounding so feeble, "we're legally separated."

"Yes, a piece of paper — a mere piece of paper — stands between us. If I liked I could rip it to pieces. And then there would be nothing between us," his eyes glinted, "not even this towel." He started to remove it, but she resisted, her face flaming. He held her rigid body against his for a few moments, then he thrust her away.

Marisa sank weakly on to the side of the bath. Her defences against him did not even have the substance of a cobweb. He strolled at last into the bedroom and she dried and dressed herself quickly.

"I suppose," he called, "you're getting agitated in case Elwyn comes."

She found him sitting in the armchair. He remarked, tormenting her, "Since I have more right here than he has, I'm staying a while. I'm sorry to thwart your plans and frustrate you for a few more hours, but Elwyn can always come back when I've gone — *if* I go."

She stopped in her tracks. "You *must* go. You haven't booked in."

"I could soon get round that. They know I'm your husband. I told them."

Desperate now, Marisa said the first thing that came into her head. "There's — there's only a single bed."

He stood in front of her, resting his hands lightly on her waist. "Come, come, you must do better than that. When has a single bed ever deterred lovers?"

"We're not lovers."

There was a hesitant tap at the door. Dirk moved away, his eyes holding something like disgust. "No, we're not, are we? A woman can hardly run to two men at the same time." He smiled cynically. "Too exhausting for words!" The tap came again. "Well, aren't you going to let him in?"

She opened the door to Elwyn. He saw Dirk standing in the background, arms folded, smiling. He floundered, "I'm — I'm sorry, Marisa. I thought you'd be alone. I was going to take you down to dinner."

"I'm taking her," Dirk said blandly, "but thanks all the same."

Marisa swung round on him. "I can choose who I like to take me to dinner. Anyway," she compromised, "I'm not hungry. I've decided against a meal."

"I've booked a table, Marisa. For two." She saw the glint in his eye and thought it prudent at least to get Elwyn off the premises.

"Thank you, Elwyn," she said soothingly, "it's very kind of you to think of me, but as Dirk's booked . . ." She did not finish the sentence. Instead, she reached up and kissed him on the mouth.

He coloured and looked nervously at Dirk as if expecting retribution. But Dirk did not move a muscle, except to smile more broadly. Elwyn smiled, too, a mollifying, placatory smile as if he were trying to soothe an angry customer complaining about an ill-cut suit. Discreetly he withdrew.

Marisa turned, prepared to face Dirk's anger, but he was laughing softly. "What was that supposed to be – a consolation prize? If a girl kissed me like that, I'd call it an insult."

She thought it expedient to draw his mind away from the subject. "If you insist on taking me to dinner –"

"I do."

"Then I'll have to change into something more suitable."

"Go ahead." She looked at him doubtfully. "What are you waiting for? You don't really expect me to turn my back while you take your dress off?" He approached her, smiling. "Perhaps you need help?"

"No, thank you." She moved away quickly.

At the bottom of her case she found the only expensive dress she had ever bought. Its vivid red velvet top was long-sleeved and its deep cut-out neckline was repeated at the back. The skirt was of bright tartan taffeta, the red in it matching the top exactly.

She shook it free of creases and draped it across the bed.

Dirk folded his arms and leant against the wardrobe, watching as she peeled off her working dress and threw it on a chair. With fingers made awkward by the interest in his eyes, she drew the other dress over her head. The zip at the back proved difficult to reach and he wandered slowly across to stand behind her.

With one hand he held her shoulder, with the other he zipped up the dress. The hand on her shoulder moved to her neck and burrowed under her hair. The other hand did likewise. His lips rested for a long moment against the bare skin revealed by the lifting of her hair. Marisa held her breath.

Then, as if it were an everyday occurrence, he walked away. When she turned to face him, her skin stinging as if she had received a burn, his eyes revealed no emotion, no disturbance, no expression at all.

"Mind if I use the phone?" It stood on the bedside table. He sat on the bed, reached out for the receiver and dialed the number. Then he sank back against the pillows.

When the call was answered he said, "Luella? Dirk here. Sorry I can't join you for dinner tonight. Something unexpected has cropped up. I'll be engaged for the next hour or two." He listened. "Come later? Yes, I could probably do that. I've started on the plans and I'll show you what I've done so far. How's Patrick? He was waiting up for me? Tell him I'm sorry to disappoint him. I'll see him next time. Tomorrow?" He turned and asked Marisa, who was mechanically applying make-up at the dressing-table, "Is there a rehearsal tomorrow evening? There is? Sorry, Luella, can't be done. All right, day after tomorrow. Yes, I'll come to dinner. Thanks, I'll look forward to it. 'Bye."

He moved to stand beside her and watched as she applied eye-shadow to her already shadowed eyes. She cleared her throat because it seemed reluctant to function. "You could have missed the rehearsal if your—business was all that important."

He said nothing. She pursued the subject, trying to force him to react and at the same time to purge herself of jealousy. "It's a shame to disappoint the little boy. You need not take me to dinner." He stayed silent. She turned to him, her heart breaking, "Go and see your future stepson, I don't mind."

He remained passive. "Are you ready to go down?"

But her jealousy superseded her common sense. "You'll have a rich wife, won't you? And beautiful as well. Since I'm neither, why don't you divorce me? Then you could marry her."

61

His hand found her shoulder again. His fingers pressed into her flesh, impelling her towards the door. "You know my condition for a divorce."

"And if I refuse to comply?"

"Then we remain as we are, with you tied to me until the requisite time has passed for you to apply to the courts claiming irretrievable breakdown of marriage. But I would almost certainly contest it. I'd get my lawyer to cite the generous way I'm treating you financially, the frequency with which we see each other, our collaboration in outside activities." He smiled gratingly. "So you see, I'd make it very, very difficult for you. Who, after that, could call such a marriage irretrievably broken?"

"But," she turned and put her back to the door, refusing to allow him to open it, "what would you get out of doing that? It would mean you wouldn't be free, either. Without a divorce you couldn't marry again."

"What does it matter these days if a man isn't 'free' as you put it? Most women don't give it another thought. If they want a man –"

"And Luella wants you?"

"That I have yet to find out. Our relationship hasn't progressed far enough for me to know."

"But it will?" She was like a desperate person who had turned a revolver towards her own heart.

"It may do. Isn't that what you want me to say?"

Together they went down to dinner.

The chandeliers glinted over the diners, the soft-footed waiters hovered, the sweet music cajoled and coaxed even the most agitated into near-serenity. The miseries of the day, the feeling of homelessness, of being abandoned and unwanted, retreated behind a closed door in Marisa's mind. Later, in the darkness, when sleep would not come, she knew her worries would creep out to trouble her like the frightening ghost images of childhood.

But all that mattered at the moment was that for the first time ever, she was dining with her husband. During the whole of their two years together, they had not been able to afford it.

62

Now, ironically, when they had parted, the money was there, but the love was not.

"Dirk?" He looked up, pausing in the act of eating. "What am I going to do about the furniture and everything else the bailiffs dumped outside?" She was appealing to him helplessly, revealing how dependent on him she still was.

"I've taken care of that. I contacted a removal firm, and impressed on them the urgency of the situation. After you left, I supervised the loading of the stuff on to their van. They're drying it out and storing it."

His thoughtfulness overwhelmed her and she expressed her gratitude haltingly.

"You'll have to find somewhere to live," he said. "A furnished flat would be best."

"I was thinking of a couple of rooms."

"But why?" His tone was sharp. "I've increased your maintenance allowance. You're earning a reasonable salary. You could afford something better."

"Flats are hard to find."

"Sorry, now, you turned down the one I found for you?"

"Perhaps."

He smiled. "You know damned well you are. If I hear of another I'll let you know. In the meantime, you can continue to live here."

"I can't do that." She was aghast. "The cost would be beyond me. It's the most expensive hotel in town."

"I'm paying for this, Marisa."

She did rebel then. "You're not! I can't allow that. It would cost a fortune for me to stay here. A luxury bedroom, private bathroom –" She shook her head. "I'll move into a cheaper place."

"You still can't forget the past, can you, when we had to skimp and scrape and do without? Times have changed. I'll tell you in confidence that Mr. Hilsby is retiring in a few weeks, and I'm becoming Mr. Garner's partner. The name of the firm will be changed to Garner, Sterling and Associates." She had suspected that. "Mr. Garner is already paying me a partner's salary, even before I've officially taken up the position." He pushed away his empty plate. "I'm not poor any more, Marisa."

"All the same, I can't allow you to subsidise me twice over. An allowance plus hotel charges."

"You are staying here, Marisa, for as long as is necessary, and at my expense." He spoke quietly and with emphasis. "The matter is settled."

She said, "Thank you," but the words seemed so inadequate in the face of his generosity that a sense of guilt created by her indebtedness to him brought the colour to her cheeks.

He smiled and put out his hand, covering hers momentarily. "It's odd, isn't it, that you should be embarrassed by your husband's benevolence? But it suits you."

When the meal was over she asked him, "How did you know what had happened this afternoon?"

"Jan rang me. As soon as I heard, I acted." He smiled, cynical now. "I knew you would be hopeless at organising anything and would go running straight to beloved Elwyn – which you did. I also knew he'd be as helpless as you."

She said indignantly, "I didn't go running to him. He was there and –"

"And provided a convenient shoulder to cry on." He smiled reminiscently. "You never were a woman of action, were you?"

Upstairs in her room again he asked, putting his hands on her arms and baiting her a little, "Don't I merit a 'thank you' kiss after all I've done today? You kissed Elwyn for nothing. What about me?"

"Don't be silly." She backed away, but he followed. "I can't kiss you. Not now. We're separated. I – I do thank you, though. I can't say how much."

He persisted, holding on to her again. "You can *show* how much." He pulled her close. "Come on." His lips approached hers, but she held back.

"No."

Dirk lifted a hand and took her face between his palms. He lowered his head and rested his mouth against hers. "My word,"

64

he whispered, when he had finished, "I'm tempted to stay. Very tempted indeed."

"No, no. You mustn't. I'm your estranged wife —" She felt her ability to withstand him fading like daylight on a winter's day. She closed her eyes and darkness came suddenly. She wanted him to kiss her, and his arms to crush away her resistance.

"I'm not thinking of you as my wife. I'm thinking of you as a woman, an enticing, attractive woman."

It was like a blinding light being switched on to torture her as if she were a prisoner under interrogation. To him all she was now was just "another woman."

She twisted away from him with violence. "You haven't 'bought' me just because you're paying for me to stay here. If that's the way you want me to show my gratitude, then the sooner I move out of this hotel, the better. Anyway, you have an appointment to keep."

He held on to his temper with difficulty. "Don't worry, I'm not staying. Did you really think I would make it so easy for you to gain your freedom? And afterwards you could go running to Elwyn and tell him, 'Soon we'll be able to marry?' " He said the cruellest thing he could think of. "I'm going to Luella. She'll welcome me with open arms. And I mean open arms."

When he had gone, Marisa sank on the bed and let her emotions take over.

When Jan saw Marisa next morning, she said,

"We wondered what had happened to you, so Neville phoned Dirk to find out if you needed any help. So you're installed at the Carlton? Only the best for you!" she laughed.

"At Dirk's insistence, and expense. I argued, but it wasn't any use."

"Why argue? You're still his wife and to a certain extent you're still his responsibility, especially in his present circumstances. Now he's one of the 'high-ups' he can't have his wife living in near poverty, can he? You know how gossip spreads, even in a sizeable town like this one."

"You mean it would be bad for his public image if he neglected me? And good for it, and for business, if it got around how well he was treating his estranged wife? Yes, I do see what you mean. That explains a lot."

Her heart was breaking to pieces, slowly, like a ship cast up on the rocks. Any hope she might have had deep inside her that he might have been doing it out of regard, if not love, for her capsized and sank.

"It could also," she reflected, "twist round the truth in the eyes of the public. It could make them think I was the guilty one and had broken up our marriage, and that he was the injured party. Yes, very clever of him."

"My dear," said Jan, upset now at what appeared to have been a *faux pas* on her part, "don't get me wrong. I didn't mean that at all."

"All the same," Marisa said wearily, "it's probably true."

Greg Johnson swept into the room, talking to all the girls in turn, finishing up, as Marisa knew he would, at her desk. "I'll say it for you – long time no see. I've been away on a course. Now I'm back to pester you. When are you coming out with me?"

Marisa laughed, her mood lightening as it always did in Greg's company. "I suppose I'll have to one day, if only to keep you quiet."

"You never spoke a truer word. Name the day."

She shook her head, smiling. "I'll have to consult my appointments diary. I'm a busy woman these days. I've got a play to produce."

"Amateur drama, eh? Tell me when it's on, I'll come and see it. But seriously, I'd like to take you out."

She tried putting him off. "Soon, Greg, soon, I promise."

He went away, satisfied for the moment.

She did not see Dirk until the rehearsal that evening. He was there when she walked in with Elwyn. He did not greet her with the others but held back, a sardonic smile on his face, and waited for her to go to him.

Marisa approached, smiling uncertainly. "Hallo, Dirk." He inclined his head, his eyes mocking.

66

She had to remember that amongst these people her connection with him was not known. They were supposed only to be acquaintances.

Sally rushed in. "Sorry I'm late, everyone." She made straight for Dirk, elbowing Marisa out of the way. "Hi, Dirk." She reached up and kissed him on the cheek. Everyone laughed, knowing Sally.

"What's that for?" Dirk asked, enjoying himself.

"That's to show you I like you."

"As if I didn't know," he joked. His smile was directed spitefully at Marisa.

Reluctantly Sally left him to join the rest of the cast on the stage. Marisa sat with the others in the centre of the hall. Dirk talked quietly to Norman, planning the scenery, making sketches, comparing notes.

"Let's take it from the beginning," Marisa called. The rehearsal started, but it took the cast some time to warm up.

Halfway through, Anna, whose job was costumes, went into the small kitchen behind the stage and made them all a cup of tea. While they drank it, they discussed the play.

When they resumed the rehearsal, Marisa said, "Let's have the love scene between Courtenay and Alys. You both know most of the words, so you can put your books away and we'll have some action."

Elwyn, who had had secondary roles in the past, had not yet been able to lose himself in the part of the leading man. He was stiff and unconvincing and could not throw off his irritating self-consciousness.

Marisa, fighting to keep her patience, said, "This is supposed to be a passionate love scene, Elwyn. You must forget the audience. Imagine there's a wall between you and them and that you're alone with Sally."

There was a movement at her side and she saw that Dirk had taken the seat next to her. He taunted in Marisa's ear, "What wouldn't I give to be alone with Sally!"

She ignored him and called out, "Let's have the bit leading up to the kiss."

Obediently they carried out the actions and Sally, doing he best to give Elwyn a lead, nestled up to him trying to draw som simulated warmth from him. He put his arms round her awk wardly and kissed her.

"Is that how he kisses you when you're alone?" Dirk whis pered. "Good grief, when you're married to him, you'll hav to feed him on a diet of unadulterated aphrodisiac to bring ou his desires!"

Sally grew desperate and looked round the hall. "Can't some one *show* him how to do it?"

"Any offers?" asked Matt, laughing. "Me, for instance?" H got up, but Dirk pushed him aside.

"I'll show him how," he said, sprinting up the stairs and o to the stage. "Come on, young Sally. You've been asking fo this."

He seized her and kissed her, bending her back until she ha to cling to him. When he let her go, she was breathless, but he eyes were shining. "Wow," she gasped, "can you kiss!"

"Years of practice," he remarked carelessly, "nothing to Well, Elwyn, get the idea?"

Dirk returned to his seat with a satisfied grin. "Did that brin back memories?" he whispered to Marisa.

"No, it did *not*!" she choked, knowing full well that she wa lying. She recovered herself, saying aloud, "Now you, Elwy Try it again, will you?"

This time, as if Dirk's challenge had loosened his muscle his attempt at kissing was more successful.

"See what I've done for you?" Dirk whispered tauntingl "After this, he'll be able to kiss you properly in private!"

When the rehearsal was over, Dirk suggested to Norman tha they should meet some time at his flat to discuss the scenery an lighting, and Norman agreed.

Sally made sure it was Dirk who took her home. She hung o to his arm, gazing up at him, and he visibly wallowed in he admiration.

"Goodnight, Marisa," he said with a mocking smile. "Happ dreams!"

68

Elwyn took Marisa back to the hotel. He lingered, probably hoping she would invite him in, but he was disappointed. His kiss before he left her was more passionate than usual, and Marisa reflected that he had learned his lesson well.

Greg sought Marisa out at work and said he was sorry to hear she was temporarily homeless. "Too bad they threw you out. Do you know they're demolishing the houses tomorrow? Heard it on the grapevine."

"No," Marisa answered miserably, "I didn't know."

Next day she had a quick lunch, excusing herself from Jan and telling her where she was going. When she saw the demolition contractors at work, she felt as if she were witnessing a public execution. It was like seeing herself gunned down by a firing squad.

A group of people had gathered, and in her jaundiced state of mind, Marisa compared them with a flock of circling vultures anticipating the death of their prey.

An elderly man came to stand beside her. He said, "Another bit of the old town coming down."

Marisa gave a grudging "Yes," feeling disinclined to talk. But he went on, nodding to the great blocks of offices which lined the road,

"Did you know this part before they got going on them?"

"I used to live here," she answered shortly. "They got us out. Compulsory purchase."

The old man was sympathetic. "Used to be a builder myself, so I can understand the Council wanting to get their hands on this land. They weren't very nice houses, were they, miss?"

"It was home to me."

"That's always the sad part," the man admitted, "the human side. But we all have to give way to progress in the end, I suppose."

"How long will it take," she asked, making use of the man's professional knowledge, "to knock them down?"

"Well, now, first the demolition contractors have to make preparations. They don't go barging in with the bulldozers. It's all

69

carefully thought out beforehand. Every bit of material that's taken out of the building can be sold, and that means more profit for the contractors. If you have a good look you can see they've already taken away all the doors, windows, timber and pipes, everything that's not necessary for holding up the walls. They've taken off the roof, bit by bit, too. All that stuff's been sent away as it was taken down, so nothing got mixed up together – you know, like steel with wood, and so on. When nothing else is left, they come along and knock it inwards. They'll probably do that today. You can see the bulldozer and crane over there standing ready. Then the lorries come and cart the stuff away. They can sell the rubble, too. It's used as hard core to put underneath the foundations of buildings."

In a sense, Marisa thought, her heart lifting a little, the house lives on in other ways, other buildings, like someone who leaves part of himself after he's died for transplant into other human beings.

With a smile she thanked him for his information and he lifted his hand in a salute, saying he'd enjoyed talking to her and she mustn't get too upset about it because the old always had to make way for the new. "That's life," he said. "After all, look at me, I retired and someone younger took over from me!" He wandered away.

As Marisa watched him go, her eye was caught by a familiar figure standing a few yards from her. It was Dirk, and her heart throbbed with something like anger at the sight of him. She supposed Jan had told him where she had gone.

The old man had been right. The crane was manoeuvred into position and its long arm moved round. Attached to it was a thick, heavy chain with a large metal ball on the end of it. The arm moved, the chain swung like a giant pendulum and the ball was sent crashing against the walls of the houses. Some of the brickwork went tumbling inside. The crane shifted, the chain swung again, and again the ball pounded remorselessly against the walls. More bricks went flying.

The crane moved once more and took up its position outside

the house that used to be hers and Dirk's. Marisa turned away, sickened, unable to stand the sight of the shattered walls, the jagged empty shell, the final collapse.

Now Dirk was beside her and she turned on him, speaking softly so that no one else could hear. "Why have you come? To make sure no part of our past was left standing and that not even a brick remained? It's symbolic of our marriage, isn't it? Nothing left, not even a memory." She controlled the waver in her voice. "Are you gloating over the part you're going to play in putting up a concrete and glass monstrosity in its place? I suppose you're already thinking out the design for yet another monument to your architectural genius?"

He answered calmly, "I'm sorry, but I can't get emotional about a pile of rubble."

"Is that all you think of it?" The words were thick with tears. "It was our home, wasn't it? We were happy there . . ."

"Were we?" His voice was toneless. "Which is presumably why we drifted apart. Be honest and admit our marriage was a calamity and that after a few months of heaven, we came down to earth and discovered we were incompatible."

The houses were almost gone, the bulldozer was moving in to finish the job. People were drifting back to work after their lunch hour.

Marisa's voice rose. "We were not incompatible. We could have been happy if you'd let us, if you hadn't worked and worked –"

"And you hadn't left me every evening for Elwyn Worrell's company."

"We were young then. Now we're older . . ."

He turned to her. "What exactly are you trying to do – persuade me to come back to you, to take up our marriage where we left off?"

With a shock she realised that what she had been saying could easily have been interpreted by him in that way. Was it, in fact, what she had been trying to do?

71

"*You* come back to *me*?" she cried. "If the thought didn't horrify me so much, I'd laugh till I cried!" She had had her own back for the cruelty of his words. She walked off, her miser tearing her apart.

CHAPTER V

WHEN Marisa was having her lunch next day, Greg left the others and sat beside her. As usual, Jan had chosen a table next to her husband's. Marisa was aware that Dirk could hear everything Greg was saying.

"How about breaking your vow of abstinence from my company and coming out with me tonight?"

She could not say there was a rehearsal, because there wasn't. Nor could she say she was otherwise engaged. At the hotel there was nothing to do in the evenings. Last night Dirk had gone to Luella Ackland's. Tonight why shouldn't she, Marisa, go out with Greg?

"Come on," he said, taking advantage of her hesitation, "be a devil. Come to a show."

"Well, yes, thanks, Greg . . ."

She stole a look at Dirk, hoping he had not heard, but he must have done, because when she glanced at him he was smiling sardonically at the sauce bottle he had picked up from the table, and was reading its label with concentrated interest.

"Right seven-thirty, the Carlton, to pick up one Mrs. Marisa Sterling."

Swaggering a little, he returned to the men's table and looked at Dirk. "Got a date tonight," he whispered loudly to one of the others, "a date I've been chasing for weeks."

Later, Dirk sent for her. Feeling as guilty as if she had broken the law, she went upstairs to him. He gave her a scathing look. "So you're going out with Greg Johnson?"

"Yes, why not? I can do what I like with my private life. As you said about yourself, I don't have to ask permission to have men friends."

He declined to answer the challenge in her words and transferred his eyes to the papers in front of him, handing a few sheets to her. "These are some schedules of specifications. I'd like them typed as soon as possible."

Marisa took them without a word and returned to her desk.

Greg called for her in his modest secondhand car. She was ready for him in the hotel entrance foyer and he followed her out, joking about how the shabbiness of his car made it conspicuous among all the other expensive models parked around it.

They went to a show and in the interval they had a sandwich and a drink at the bar. Greg asked her tentatively, "How are things between you and Dirk?"

She shrugged. "The same. We're as wide apart as ever."

"Can't you divorce him?"

"It's difficult. We both signed a deed agreeing to separate, which apparently precludes divorce on the grounds of desertion. If one of the couple wants a divorce and the other doesn't, there's nothing the one who wants it can do, unless he or she can persuade the other to agree. It's just a matter of waiting for the necessary time to pass, when apparently you can be granted a divorce on the grounds of 'irretrievable breakdown of the marriage.'"

"In other words, for the moment he's got you in a spot?"

She shrugged again, not wishing to go into details.

He offered her some crisps. "Coming to the firm's annual dinner? I did hear a rumour that Mr. Hilsby's returning for it and they're going to announce his retirement. They'll also be asking for contributions to his retirement present." He made a face. "No doubt a memo will come round that 'all are expected to give generously.'"

"In that case I suppose I shall have to go to the dinner."

"Your husband's rumoured to be his successor. Did you know?"

"Yes. He told me 'in confidence.' He should have known nothing can be kept secret for long."

"Well, he's been occupying Hilsby's room, hasn't he, since the old boy went on holiday? That was a give-away in itself." He put his arm round her. "Now he's being promoted, doesn't

74

that make you want to heal the breach and get together with him again?"

Marisa did not answer his question directly. She frowned. "To me love is more important than money and position."

"Well said, madam. I'd take my hat off to you if I wore one. It also lets me know where I stand."

She laughed. "Ah, but you don't know about Elwyn Worrell. He's next in line to marry me, or so he thinks."

"My little sweetie," he kissed her ear, "who's talking about marriage?"

The bell rang, indicating the end of the interval and with relief Marisa led the way to their seats. When the play was over, they went out into the cold and the darkness. During the evening some snow had fallen and it lay on the roof of Greg's car like a thin glistening blanket.

He drove to the hotel and parked outside. "The bar won't be closed yet," he said, looking at his watch, "let's have a drink or two."

Marisa agreed and they pushed through the swing doors, stamping the snow from their shoes. Greg took her coat and held it over his arm. She patted her hair, feeling the dampness caused by the snowflakes which had settled on it outside.

"Hallo, Marisa."

She raised her eyes and opened her mouth with shock. Dirk, glass in hand, was leaning against the doorway to the cocktail bar. He smiled sardonically from her to Greg and back.

Greg gave Dirk a look of concentrated hatred, which he muted to a travesty of a smile. "Hi, Dirk. Fancy seeing you here."

"Just fancy," said Dirk with a grin.

Greg tried to push past him as though he were a stranger blocking the way.

"What are you having, Marisa? Greg?" Dirk asked, forestalling Greg's question and putting him into the position of guest instead of host.

"I'll get them," Greg growled, but Dirk was at the bar, leaning against it and waiting for their answers.

"Sherry, Marisa? That's your usual, isn't it? You see, I

haven't forgotten. You, Greg? What are you going to have?"

Greg told him and he ordered.

"Find a seat, Marisa," Dirk told her, taking the initiative again. "Keep one for me."

"Why didn't you tell me he'd be here?" Greg demanded, sitting beside her and putting her coat on the back of her chair.

"How could I, when I didn't know myself?" she snapped.

Greg said, nodding towards Dirk, "Is he staying the night?"

"Of course not! I told you how things are between us."

"I'm beginning to wonder," Greg muttered.

Dirk was making his way towards them, carrying the drinks on a tray. She said quietly, "Thank you for this evening, Greg. I really did enjoy it."

"At least one of us did, then."

She touched his hand with hers. "Don't be like that, Greg, please."

Dirk set the tray down on the small round table and placed the glasses on the circular mats in front of them. "Well," he said heartily, "did you enjoy your evening out?"

Greg remained silent, so Marisa filled in the awkward pause.

"Very much thank you. The play was good, wasn't it, Greg?"

Greg nodded and took a long drink. His frown looked as though it was fixed to his face with glue. Marisa gave him up and turned to Dirk.

"Why did you come?"

He could not resist a smile. "To – er – have a word with you. About the play."

Greg drained his glass and set it down with a thump. "I'm off." To Marisa, "See me out?"

"Will you excuse me?" she asked Dirk coldly.

He nodded. "But hurry back, darling."

She lifted her head a little higher and followed Greg outside. He put on his coat and took her hand, pulling her behind him.

"What was that 'darling' business?"

"He only said it to annoy," she soothed. "That's Dirk all over."

He was like a disappointed small boy and, without asking,

kissed her goodnight with as much petulance as passion, but she submitted without resistance, feeling a little sorry for him.

When he had gone she returned to the hotel to find Dirk waiting in the entrance hall. It seemed he was determined not to let her slip away from him up to bed.

"Come in here." He propelled her back into the bar.

"It's late," she protested. "They'll be closing in a minute."

"You're a resident. They won't turn you out. We can talk here."

"There's nothing to talk about. Why aren't you honest and admit you only came to spy on me?"

"You're so right, darling," he mocked. "I came to act as your bodyguard," his eyes flicked over her, "in the literal sense of the word." He finished his drink. "Of course, the unknown factor was what your reaction would be to my appearance. But I took a chance on that."

She said sarcastically, "I thank you from the bottom of my heart. I'll do the same for you some time, when you take Luella out."

Dirk threw back his head and laughed. "That," he said, still enjoying the thought, "will be the day."

"Did you really want to see me?"

"Believe it or not, I did. Tomorrow evening Norman is coming to my place to discuss the scenery. We need the co-operation of the producer, so will you join us?"

"At your flat? You've never even given me your address."

"Haven't I? We must remedy that at once. My dear wife, let me give you my card." With a flourish he found one and handed it to her. "With your husband's compliments." She put it in her handbag. "Absurd, isn't it – a wife not knowing where her husband lives! Well, can you make it?"

"Yes, I think so."

"Good. I'll draw you a map." He found a scrap of paper. "I love drawing maps. Come closer and I'll explain as I go." She moved along the seat and peered over his shoulder as he named the roads and directed her. He turned towards her cheek. "I like your perfume."

"It was a Christmas present."

"Don't tell me — from Elwyn." She nodded. "I hate your perfume."

She laughed, taking the map. "What time shall I arrive?"

"Any time. Come to a meal. It's a service flat. I don't do the cooking."

"No, thanks."

He shrugged. "Please yourself."

Marisa yawned. "I'm tired. Mind if I go to bed?" She picked up her handbag.

"See me on the premises?" She put on her coat and went outside with him. "I suppose you kissed Greg goodnight?"

"I had to," she excused herself. "He was so disappointed to find you here."

He looked down at her in the darkness, his expression unreadable in the shadow.

"And were you?"

She thought it best to prevaricate. "I have no feelings on the subject."

"You," he said tightly, catching her wrists and jerking her close, "sorely tempt me to provoke you into having some feelings on the subject."

His fingers were bruising her flesh, but she endured the pain rather than let him know he was hurting her. There was a brief pause and she held her breath. Was he going to kiss her?

But he let her go. "Goodnight, Marisa," he said, and went away.

When Marisa arrived at Dirk's flat the following evening, Norman opened the door. Dirk, he explained, was spread all over the dining room table drawing plans. "He's in his element. He's submerged in paper and yet more paper, and I can't supply him with enough pencils."

Marisa nearly said, "That brings back memories," but stopped herself just in time.

"It's the architect in me," Dirk called. "I see everything in terms of diagrams, plans and drawings."

"Even women?" Norman asked.

"In a way, yes," came the answer. "When I think of a woman I think of shapes and curves." He looked up as they entered. "But I've never planned a woman. Buildings, yes, women no. It might be quite a challenge – planning the perfect woman, from basic. The idea intrigues me." He eyed Marisa lingeringly and returned to his sketching. "Well, Marisa, do you approve of my flat?"

"So far, yes. I like your impressive entrance hall."

"The entrance hall," Dirk pronounced, "is the most ridiculous waste of space imaginable. The architect who designed these flats needed a refresher course. Who wants a large hall, anyway? Except, as you've just said, to impress. Have a look round. Imagine it's yours and that you're sharing it with a man." He gave her a wicked smile. "With me, if you like."

Their eyes clashed and Marisa withdrew hers first. As she walked from the dining-room through the connecting door into the kitchen, she let out a sigh of envy. "What a beautiful kitchen!"

He joined her. "It's got everything, hasn't it? All the latest gadgets, and a man to go with it." He grinned. "The bedroom's pretty good, too. It's even got a double bed. Any offers?"

Norman laughed from the dining-room. "You're a fast worker, Dirk. You haven't known Marisa for more than a few weeks and here you are making improper suggestions!" They laughed, exchanging secret smiles. "Anyway," Norman went on, "judging by what I know of her, I doubt if you'll find Marisa that sort of girl."

"No?" said Dirk, softly, disbelievingly.

They returned to the dining-room. "No," Marisa said firmly. "I've been married before, don't forget." She looked straight at Dirk. "Once bitten, twice shy."

Dirk frowned. "You surprise me. Here you are, spurning the matrimonial state, and here am I, a bachelor, and completely innocent where that sort of thing's concerned, thinking marriages are made in heaven." He gave Marisa a secret sarcastic look and resumed his work.

79

She said a little sharply, and looking over his shoulder, "What are you doing?"

"Making a plan of how I'm going to use the stage 'flats'. Norman tells me there are a stock of them already backstage at the hall."

"There are. We've used them before. They're getting just a bit tattered with constant use. The canvas which covers the wood is torn in one or two places."

"I can soon mend those."

Norman watched him for a moment. "You remember there are a couple of windows in the drawing-room scene, one a casement and one a french window?"

Dirk nodded. "I'll hang a rectangular piece of canvas behind the windows from a batten and paint the necessary scenery on the canvas to give the audience an impression of a view." He sketched for a few moments. "Now, Norman, about the lighting."

"Well, although it's supposed to be a large room, you can't light it as you would a proper room. You probably know that the main purpose of lighting in a play is to illuminate the actors? That way you focus the audience's attention on them."

"What about spotlights? I thought they were important."

"Yes, they are. I use those a lot, too. In fact, most of the lighting comes from spotlights, and I place them at an angle of about forty-five degrees. It's most effective."

"Norman's good," Marisa said appreciatively. "Even when an actor hasn't been up to scratch, he's helped the play along in the past with his lighting."

"Glad to hear it," said Dirk. "He can cover any mistakes I might make in the scenery! Are there by any chance a stock of doors, windows, fireplaces and so on?" Norman nodded. "What a pity! I was hoping I'd have to design some myself. I love making three-dimensional pieces for the stage."

"I didn't know you'd done that sort of work," Marisa said, her tone rebuking him a little for keeping such a thing a secret.

He looked up quickly and frowned, cautioning her. "How could you, when I haven't known you very long?"

She coloured slightly and said, "Oh, of course not."

"Come closer," said Dirk to Marisa. "Now this is what I had in mind. You'll see I've sketched the setting as it will appear to the audience. Can you see what I'm getting at?"

"I think so." She fingered the paper he was using. "I seem to recognise this stuff."

"You should. It's draughtsman's tracing paper, the sort of thing you see lying about at the office. I bought a few sheets and used it so that copies can be run off easily. You'll need a copy, so will Norman, for the lighting effects. Matt will need one to help him stage-manage, and I'll want one myself."

"My word," said Norman, "this is really going to be a professional production. We've never had anyone as particular as you helping us before."

Dirk smiled. "It's in my blood – and my training as an architect. I never like to omit the details and," looking at Marisa, "I never like to leave a job unfinished. It irks me. I regard it as a challenge I've failed to meet."

She moved away, telling herself that she was imagining the hidden meaning behind his words, but Dirk said, "Come back here, Madam Producer." She returned to his side. "Don't you realise how important it is for the two of us to understand each other? There should be constant consultation between the designer and the producer. It's vital to the success of the production. Bring up a chair, sit next to me." He smiled mockingly. "You're not afraid of me, are you? I don't bite. Only women bite – usually the men they love."

Norman laughed, "You seem to know a lot about women, Dirk. Where did you learn it?"

"Oh," he looked at Marisa sitting beside him, "I've knocked about the world. Had a number of girl-friends."

She stared at him. What was he talking about? The man she had married had been a quiet, studious young man, dedicated to his work and short-tempered with anyone who got in the way of it, as she knew to her cost. He must have been fooling, just to provoke her.

"Come on, Norman," Dirk said, "let's study these plans."

"Here," said Norman sitting beside him, "under the french windows, there's a chaise-longue, and a mirror of the same period. I'll try to fix the lighting so that it catches the mirror and reflects back on to the chaise-longue while the passionate love scene is taking place."

"Talking of passion, Marisa," Dirk digressed with a grin, "how's Elwyn shaping up with his kissing?"

She smiled back provocatively. "Do you mean in public or in private?"

He bared his teeth at her momentarily, knowing Norman would not be able to see the intimate piece of by-play.

"In public, of course."

"He's coming on. You see, I'm giving him lessons. In private."

This time he lifted his hand and tugged her hair. She squealed. "Now now, you two," Norman reprimanded. "This is business. Pleasure comes later."

"Hear that, Marisa? Does it?" Dirk smiled again.

"Definitely no." She pointed to the diagrams. "You were saying?"

"She's putting me back on course, as a good secretary should. Did you know, Norman, she's my secretary at work?"

"No, I didn't." Norman looked interested. "That's why you seem to know each other so well, then."

"Yes," said Dirk, suddenly vague, "it must be."

They discussed the scenery for some time, then Dirk said, "I feel like some refreshments. Care to act the hostess and make some, Marisa? You can have the run of my kitchen." As she rose, he smiled provocatively. "Just pretend you're in your own home."

"Home is where the heart is," Marisa said tritely, "and," she turned away so that Dirk could not see her face as she lied, "my heart isn't here."

"She's got a boy-friend, Dirk, that's obvious. You're too late, mate."

She closed the sliding door into the kitchen so that she would not have to hear Dick's reply. There were biscuits and cakes in tins in the cupboards, cutlery in drawers and crockery on shelves.

Marisa made the coffee, piled the trolley with the food and drink and wheeled it through the doorway into the dining-room.

As they ate and drank, they pored over Dirk's plans. "Who's going to do the painting?" Norman asked.

"Me, of course," said Dirk. "I love sloshing paint all over blank surfaces!"

"But it's not as simple as that, is it?" Norman remarked.

"No, I was exaggerating a little. Did you know that even in a real room each wall reflects the light differently, and you can even get a variation of light reflected from a single wall? To make a stage 'room' look realistic, the painter has to try to get this effect, and do it so cunningly the audience won't consciously notice."

"You seem to know quite a bit about it," Marisa commented. "Have you done a lot of this sort of thing?"

"In the past – er – let me see, three years, I've spent a great deal of my leisure time helping out amateur drama groups. It kept my mind off my problems and," Dirk smiled irritatingly, "it passed the time between girl-friends."

Marisa held in her agitation and gathered the empty cups. She wheeled them into the kitchen and started washing them up.

Norman said he must be off. He put his head into the kitchen.

" 'Bye, Marisa, see you at the next rehearsal.'"

Dirk saw him out, then returned to lean against the kitchen doorway. "Just like old times. No one would believe it if we told them our marriage had broken down, would they?"

Marisa said, trying to freeze him, "I'm here as the producer of the play, visiting you as the artistic director."

"Strictly business."

"Exactly."

"Leave those and come and sit down. You haven't got to go yet. The hotel won't lock you out."

He led her into the lounge which was comfortably furnished

and warm from the central heating. She settled with a sigh into an armchair and took the drink he offered: He sat opposite her.

"You have a nice home, Dirk."

He said, as though there were no argument, "It's not a home. It's simply a place to live."

"How did you find the Midlands?"

He shrugged. "If you mean the office, it was reasonably flourishing. There's a lot of redevelopment going on in those parts. New shopping centres, public amenities and so on. Invaluable experience for me. But the area —" He shook his head. "I missed the northern hills and fells. I missed them so much I wanted to come back to them." He looked outside at the blackness and realised he had not pulled the curtains. He did so, returning to his chair. "I'm longing for the spring and summer when I can get on to the moors again. Winter imprisons one, doesn't it? There's all that beauty almost within touching distance, and here I am, shut in by brick and concrete, not to mention the foul weather we've been having ever since my return."

She murmured, staring into the imitation log fire he had switched on, "I think the moors in winter are just as beautiful as they are in summer. They're wilder, more remote, even angry sometimes." She looked at him. "You know what I mean?"

"Perhaps." He was watching her closely. "Did Elwyn take you up there?"

"A couple of times, yes. We found a pub in a little village where they gave us tea as a special favour because it was out of season."

There was a long pause and the artificial flames licked and leapt impotently, feigning a power they did not possess – the power to destroy and obliterate and reduce to ashes.

"Remember," Dirk said softly, "the inn where we spent our honeymoon? The highest inn in England, they told everybody. Miles and miles from anywhere, high up on the moors. Remember the car I borrowed and the miles we covered, and how no matter in which direction we travelled, there were moors and still more moors?"

She nodded.

"That was at least something we shared," he reflected, his eyes drawn as hers were, to the heatless flames. "A love of the moorland."

"And music," she put in.

"Yes, music. You'd have thought it was enough, wouldn't you, to help a marriage to last?"

Marisa closed her eyes. "The binding factor must have been missing, mustn't it? The 'adhesive' that gives a marriage sticking power. Love."

He got up, uncovered the record player and put on a record. "This," he said, "was our favourite. 'Nimrod' from Elgar's Enigma Variations."

They listened together and she drifted back in time, becoming the young illusioned girl she had been when they had last shared that music. The brilliant harmonies took possession of her and seemed to enter her body and fill her with their own beauty and, like a dream, she believed she was back in the past, when Dirk was really her husband, loving her, possessing her, filling her thoughts every minute of the day.

The music ended, the dream grew colourless like a winter's day, and faded into darkness. He was there, his back to her, removing the record and putting it away. He was there, but no longer part of her, separate, divided, severed for ever, like an amputated limb.

"How's Luella?"

The question bounded into the silence like a beach ball from someone else's game.

He sat down again. "Blooming. Enjoying her riches."

"And her son?"

Dirk smiled affectionately. "He's a good little lad. Partly to please him and partly to help me with the design of the house Luella wants, I made a model of it. Would you like to see it? It's in the boot of my car." Before she could answer he was out of the room.

Luella Ackland, soon to be Luella Sterling. Patrick, soon to have a new father – Dirk. Marisa played with the words like someone trying to find answers to clues to a crossword puzzle.

85

Her mind baulked, like a horse refusing to take a fence. She gave up. There were too many blank squares to fill.

Dirk returned, holding with care the model of a large house. His future home, no doubt. It was made of white card. "It's all to scale," he told her, putting it on the coffee table between them.

She leaned forward, simulating interest. "The doors move. The windows open, don't they? It's a bit like a dolls' house."

"It is, which is probably why Patrick's so intrigued." He went on to explain, "The reason we make models is because, unlike drawings, a model is three-dimensional, and as near reality as an architect can get without actually building the place he's designing. When you see the model in action, you can see any mistakes you've made. Drawings are flat and what they're meant to represent is difficult to visualise. With a model like this, you can see whether you should move a wall, enlarge a room, or put the stairs somewhere else."

She smiled. "Now I can see why you love building solid pieces of stage scenery." He smiled and put the model aside. "I can't even imagine how an architect knows where to start when he's designing a building."

"That sounds odd, coming from a woman who's been married to one! Well, here beginneth the first lesson. First we make a lot of rough sketches, rearrange them, hack them about, then throw the lot away and start again. After consulting different technical people, we get more ideas, arriving at last at the final one which solves all the problems. Then we talk to the client, show him a few plans to choose from and give him an estimate of the cost. The client, of course, must never be forgotten. He – or she – must be advised at almost every step."

"Which is why," Marisa interrupted, "you've been seeing so much of *your* client?"

He smiled. "That, woman, is a leading question. Don't delude yourself that I'm not astute enough to know it."

She looked a little embarrassed, but said nothing.

"The answer is, partly yes, partly no. The dividing line between duty and pleasure where Luella is concerned is very fine."

He added gratuitously but with intent, "She's a beautiful woman."

She burst out, provoked into bitterness, "Then why don't you divorce me, and marry her?"

Dirk looked at her and through the long, painful silence she jerked her head round and focused her eyes on the false red glow.

"In the early stages of design," he said in a rebuking tone, like a teacher bringing a pupil's attention back to the subject in hand, "when I'm thinking and discussing, I doodle and sketch as the ideas come thick and fast. You may remember from the past how the house used to be littered with scraps of paper covered by my drawings."

She nodded. "Even the bedroom."

"That," he said cryptically, "was a mistake."

"You couldn't get enough pencils, either. You used to grab every one in sight."

"I still do. It's every architect's failing. At first the drawings resemble blobs, grouped together or running into each other. They represent rooms and so on. It's in this way that ideas can stay flexible. If the design becomes too rigid too soon, it's terribly difficult fitting in anything extra, like cupboards. As soon as the design loses its fluidity and becomes rigid, it's hard to avoid putting in walls. If one wall gets moved to make a room larger, it automatically makes another room smaller, which sets up a chain reaction, as it were, and that's often the end of the design. Walls, even in the mind, are incredibly difficult to move. Even," he said softly, "between people."

She stirred uncomfortably, knowing that the wall between them would one day grow so high it would part them for ever.

"Strange, isn't it, that I'm talking to you like this now, when it's too late? If I had done it years ago, perhaps things would have been different between us. You would have understood my work, instead of hating it. Then it wouldn't have proved the barrier to our happiness that it actually was."

"There was always Elwyn," she murmured, her voice toneless.

"Yes," he gave a resigned sigh, "there was always Elwyn. There still is, isn't there?" He lened forward, clasping his hands. "Marriages may come, and marriages may go, but Elwyn goes on for ever."

She looked at her watch and exclaimed at the time. "Nearly midnight! I must go."

He found her coat and she slipped into it. At the door he took her hand, her left hand. He looked at the wedding ring he had given her, meaningless now. He fiddled with it and she wondered if he was trying to take it off – a purely psychological, almost Freudian act.

He looked at her. "Ironic, isn't it, that I'm still your next of kin?"

She snatched away her hand. "Yes, but don't let it upset you. You won't be for much longer, will you?"

His eyes narrowed a fraction and when she called "Goodnight" over her shoulder, he did not answer. She ran away from him towards her car which was waiting in the darkness.

CHAPTER VI

AFTER dining at the hotel the following evening, Marisa drove across the town to visit Elwyn's mother. She had not seen her since the eviction and was beginning to feel a little guilty. Florence, Hester Worrell's sister, let her in and she was given an affectionate welcome.

Elwyn came downstairs saying he had been learning his part in the play. He kissed her, showing off his possessiveness in front of his relatives. They glowed with pleasure and like an audience watching actors, they applauded. Florence fussed around Marisa and plumped up the cushions on the settee.

"Sit here, you two," she said, "then you can hold hands."

But, sitting beside a pink-faced Elwyn, Marisa kept her hands round her handbag. How was she getting on? they asked.

The hotel was so comfortable, she told them, she had almost forgotten how to run a home!

"I bet it's expensive, dear," said Hester.

"Yes, but Dirk – I mean my husband's – paying. And he's put up my allowance, too. He insisted."

"So I should think, dear," said Hester. "Conscience money, that's what it is. Look at the way he walked out and left you on your own to fend for yourself."

"From all I hear of him, I think he's a scoundrel," Florence stated, lowering her rather bulky shape on to an upright chair. She was grey, like her sister, but younger and more agile, being fortunate enough not to suffer from her sister's physical disability.

"Well," said Marisa, unwilling to have the man she loved so called, "it just came to a point where – where we couldn't live together any more."

"I agree with Aunt Florence," said Elwyn, moving closer and putting his arm around Marisa. "And he's still not letting you go so that you can marry again."

"That's right, Elwyn," his mother encouraged, smiling at them. "She's your girl really, isn't she? Always has been. Ever since she came to live with us as a young girl you've loved her, haven't you? Only you never told her as I said you should, and she upped and married that – that nasty bit of work. I never liked him. Too secretive he was, and much too quiet. I never trust a secretive man. You don't know what's underneath all those 'good manners', all that politeness."

"It didn't take him long, did it," his aunt put in, "to show himself in his true colours? Two years, wasn't it?"

"Elwyn's open," his mother claimed proudly. "You can see it in his face. That's how I brought him up – to be honest and fearless."

Marisa had to cover her mouth and suppress a smile – Elwyn, fearless? One thing Elwyn was – and it was something his mother would be scandalised to hear if she were ever told, which luckily was unlikely – and that was a breaker-up of marriages. She looked at him now, seeing his insipidity, his pale cheeks stained red with the excitement of her nearness, his seemingly artless, self-effacing eyes uncharacteristically bold as they gazed into hers, and she wondered once again how it had ever happened that he could have torn Dirk away from her.

Then she remembered how he would never leave her alone, how he had kept phoning her, calling round, appearing on the doorstep at the most intimate moments she and Dirk had shared – when she was sitting on his knee listening to music in the semi-darkness, with only the uncertain flickering of the fire lighting the room; when they were having a meal, or even late at night when they were preparing for bed.

She remembered that it had been his calculated persistence, his refusal ever to give in and let her go, that had done the final damage, dealt the last fatal blow which had brought about the inevitable and irreparable split.

"Never you mind," his mother was saying, "you're better off without him, dear, and that's a fact."

Elwyn grabbed a hand that had strayed from the handbag and said, "I heard of an empty flat today, Marisa. Not far from here, in a large Victorian house divided into two. It's an up-stairs flat, furnished and self-contained. The downstairs rooms are cut off by a wooden partition with a door in it across the hall, so you'd be quite on your own, only sharing the front door. How about it? I've been asking customers in the shop and to-day a woman who had come in to buy her husband a shirt told me she owned the house, so she would be your landlady. She said I was a 'nice' young man, so any friend of mine would suit her as a tenant. What do you say?"

Marisa grew excited. "It doesn't sound at all bad. When can we go and see it?"

"I'll have to arrange that. I've got the woman's phone num-ber. I'll let you know."

They had a cup of tea and chatted about Mrs. Worrell's health. They had decided to stay put for a while, Mrs. Worrell said. Time in the summer to look for somewhere else to live.

Marisa kissed Elwyn's mother goodbye and felt real affection in the way Mrs. Worrell pulled her down and kissed her back. Some day, she probably hoped, this girl she was so fond of would be her daughter-in-law. However long that might take to materialise, like her son she was willing to be patient and wait for events to take their course.

Next day Elwyn phoned her at work. "We can go and see the flat tonight," he told her. "I've got the key. I'll call for you early, say half-past six. Afterwards, Marisa, I'd like to take you to dinner at your hotel." There seemed to be a disturbance in the office behind her, but she shut her ears to it and concentrated on Elwyn's voice. "Last time I tried to take you," he was saying, "your husband stepped in."

"Thanks, Elwyn," Marisa answered, "I'd like to have dinner with you. See you about six-thirty, at the hotel. 'Bye for now."

She turned to find her husband standing at her desk. He seemed to be in a bad mood and Jan made a warning face be-hind his back.

"When you've finished discussing your private affairs in work-ing hours," he snapped, "I'd like your attention."

The other girls looked up, holding their breaths in anticipation of a marital quarrel taking place before their eyes. But they were disappointed.

Marisa looked down at her typewriter, fingering the keys. "I'm sorry," she murmured. She was, after all, his secretary and he was one of the principals of the firm.

"I've got a site meeting. I want you to come with me to take notes."

"When are you going?"

"Now. Get your coat and come out to my car. Bring your notebook and pencil."

"Oh, dear," said Jan, when he had gone, "are things that bad?"

Marisa shrugged. "I suppose he was right. But I couldn't help it. Elwyn phoned me, I didn't phone him. Jan, I've got the chance of a flat. We're going to see it tonight – Elwyn and I, I mean. It's not modern, but it would be better than nothing, which is what I've got now."

"Well, at least you'd have a place to call your own again." Jan looked at Marisa uncertainly. "I suppose you know where Dirk's taking you? To the site where your old house used to stand." Marisa frowned. "You'll have to harden yourself, dear."

"But I thought the firm developing the area had to apply for planning permission?"

"They were granted it a while back. It was a foregone conclusion, Neville said. I typed the bills of quantity Neville prepared and they were sent out to building contractors for tender. The developers have chosen a contractor now and everything's set for 'go'. I only know all this because Neville told me. He also told me to break it to you gently. Dirk's the architect for the blocks of offices going up there. It seems a bit hard on you being made to go with him. He might have been more tactful and taken another girl."

The other typists were listening – it was impossible for them not to hear – and Angela said, "I'm going with him to this conference he's attending soon. Did you know, Marisa? I hope you don't mind."

Marisa forced a laugh. "Mind? Why should I mind? You

92

know as well as everyone else in this office that we're separated."

Angela giggled. "To be honest, I'm a bit afraid of him. He's so sharp with us typists if we make a mistake or anything."

Marisa said, laughing genuinely now, "Well, he doesn't bite – I had that from his own lips the other day."

They laughed, too, and Marisa said, "I'd better go, otherwise he might bark at me, even if he doesn't bite!"

As they drove through the town, Dirk said, "I suppose you know where we're going?"

"Yes, Jan told me."

"I suppose you think I'm being sadistic in taking you there after all that's happened?"

She shrugged. "I don't expect anything else of you. You never did handle me with kid gloves."

"If you'd wanted gentle handling you shouldn't have married me. I never did wrap my words and actions around with cotton wool."

"That," she snapped, "is something I don't need telling. I learnt it by bitter experience."

After a brief silence she said, "I've got the offer of a flat."

"Oh?" His head shot round. "Where?"

"Not far from where Elwyn and his mother are living at the moment. Elwyn got it for me, through one of his customers."

"Making sure first, of course, that it was within pestering distance. What's the rent?"

"I don't know, but even if I did I wouldn't tell you. It's not your concern any more, is it?"

"Agreed. No doubt the added attraction is its nearness to Elwyn. What's the place like? Modern?"

"No, old. It's a large Victorian house converted into two separate flats. I'd have the upstairs. Elwyn and I are going to see it tonight."

"Prior to dining with him. I heard your discussion on the phone."

"What's wrong with my having dinner with him? After all, you have dinner with your wonderful client."

He smiled as he watched the road. "We're on rather more

intimate terms than merely having dinner together these days."

"What do you mean by that?"

He was silent.

"If you're trying to provoke me," she went on, clenching her fists with jealousy, "then you haven't succeeded."

"Haven't I?" he asked blandly. "Here we are." He pulled the car off the road and bumped a few yards over the churned-up mud which used to be the front gardens of the row of terraced houses. Already the building contractors had started assembling their materials and equipment. Excavators, cranes, tractors and lorries stood where the houses used to be. One excavator had started work, scooping and delving into the earth, shovelling it up and depositing it on to one of the waiting lorries. They had begun to dig out the foundations.

"Come on, Marisa, get out."

She looked with dismay at her shoes. "The mud! I'll get soaked through with all that water."

"I've got some boots in the back of the car. Some for myself and a pair the firm provides for any female who has to come and take notes. Try them on. They might fit."

He slipped on his own boots and brought the other pair to her, opening the door.

"Come on, let's take off your shoes."

"I'll do it," Marisa protested as he lifted up a foot.

But Dirk ignored her protest, saying softly, "There was a time, my sweet, when I seem to remember I took off far more than your shoes."

She coloured deeply and he smiled at the effect of his words. He slipped the boots on to her feet. "Get out and see how they feel." He took her hands and helped her out, gripping them in case she slipped on the mud. "Do they fit?"

"They're a bit large, but they'll do," she said.

"Good. Got your notebook? The foreman's over there." Still holding her hand, he led her across the mud to the man talking to the driver of a lorry.

As soon as the foreman saw Dirk he raised his hand and came towards them. Dirk introduced Marisa to the man.

"My wife," he said briefly. The foreman raised his eyebrows and said he was pleased to meet her. "She's also my secretary." The foreman nodded, his eyes dwelling for a passing moment on their clasped hands.

"The manager's over there," the foreman nodded to a man sitting in his car. The person to whom he was referring, the man in charge of the building firm that had won the contract, got out of his car and, also in boots, picked his way across the sea of mud. He greeted Dirk, who introduced Marisa again as "his wife".

A number of vans converged on the site and their drivers parked and walked across to join them. "Representatives of all the sub-contractors involved," the foreman explained to Marisa. "They've come for a briefing."

"Take notes of our conversation and discussion, Marisa. What we decide will be published as minutes."

The discussion was lengthy and the men spoke fast and it took Marisa all her time to keep up with what they were saying. The talk ranged over what had happened so far, some of the snags which had already been encountered and how they could be overcome, and their plans for the immediate future.

When Marisa thought the men would never stop talking, Dirk said, "Right, Marisa, that's all for now. We don't need you any more this morning. Go back to my car and wait for me."

But she put the notebook and pencil into her pocket and wandered away. She was making a pilgrimage to the past. She walked over the area on which she guessed her house had stood, and paused reverently for a moment, like someone visiting the grave of a loved one. The mud squelched as she walked on, slithering and slipping, righting herself with difficulty until she stood in what had once been a garden – her garden. There was a rose bush still standing, having miraculously escaped the ravages of the bulldozer. The white blooms still hung on it, withered and rusted, but she plucked one and put it to her nostrils. It had no smell now, and it flopped on its stalk, but she would take it back with her and dry it and press its withered petals between the leaves of a book.

As she turned and left behind the remains of the garden she had loved, she knew she had accepted at last that the past was irretrievable and the happiness she had once known beyond recall.

She picked her way carefully over some of the small pieces of rubble left behind by the demolition contractor. Her attention was distracted for a few seconds by the shout of one of the lorry drivers. She tripped over a brick and fell face down in the mud.

She gasped, but even as she fought with her feet to get a grip on the soaking earth and push herself upright, she slipped again full-length. Someone shouted and Dirk's attention must have been drawn to her.

He ran, slipping and sliding to pick her up. She thought he would be angry, but he was laughing. "What a sight! And what a mess!" He lifted her to her feet, holding her shoulders to steady her. Marisa stood, her arms dangling, as guilty as a child who had played truant and fallen in a muddy pond. Dirk called to the men, "That's it for this morning, I'm afraid. See you again in a couple of weeks. Must take my wife back and clean her up!"

There was a shout of sympathetic if slightly ribald laughter as he scooped her into his arms and carried her to the car. As he sat her on the seat, he saw the withered rose she was still clutching. It was covered with mud and scarcely recognisable. "What on earth –?" he began, but she cut him off defiantly.

"It's a rose. It's dead, it's dirty, but I'm taking it with me. I found it in our – my – garden. Somehow the bush was left standing."

"There must," he said, reversing and bumping off the mud on to the road, "be a moral in that somewhere, a meaning, an omen."

"I'm going to preserve it."

"How sentimental can you get? You find a dead rose on a dying bush, cover it with mud, then say you're going to keep it for ever."

"I knew you wouldn't understand. You never did." Marisa stared miserably out of the window. "Where are we going?"

"Back to the hotel so that you can change and clean yourself up." He looked at her quickly. "Your face is splashed with mud and your hair hasn't escaped, either." He parked in the hotel car park. "Got your room key? Let me have it."

Resentfully she gave it to him and picked up her shoes. "I can manage. There's no need for you to come in with me."

Dirk got out as though she had not spoken. "Let's hope there aren't too many people hanging around in the entrance foyer."

There were not, and they crept upstairs like conspirators, passing no one on their way. He opened the door of her room and she went in, crossing to the bathroom and filling a glass with water. Into it she put the dead rose, looking at it for a moment as if hoping it would come alive again.

Dirk asked, watching her with a strange compassion, "Going to have a quick bath?"

"I haven't time, have I? I must get back to work."

"In the circumstances, I don't think you need worry about that. As one of the bosses of the firm, I'll give you permission to have some time off to rehabilitate yourself."

"Thanks all the same, but I'll wash." She looked at him, wondering what he was going to do while she changed. He saw her uncertainty and laughed. "Get on with it. Strip, if you must. Don't mind me, I'm just your husband."

She removed her coat and hung it on the back of the door. Like her other clothes, it was caked with mud. When she had taken off her dress and slip, she realised she was still wearing the boots.

Dirk was watching her, smiling at the odd picture she presented. "Come on," he said, "sit on the bed. I'll take your boots off. Nothing else, I promise. Although you've got so little on now, it wouldn't make much difference if I did, would it?" He removed the boots and straightened, looking down at her. His eyes were shadowed and she wished they were not.

He pulled her up and into his arms. His kiss was long, intoxicating and drained her of life. His hands lingered on her bare midriff. "What man," he whispered, could resist a woman in that state of dress?"

He released her and she walked unsteadily to the bathroom. He stood beside her as she turned on the taps. "Want any help with washing?"

Marisa shook her head emphatically, still unable to trust herself to speak. He sat in a chair and read a magazine which was lying on a table.

She washed and changed, combed her hair, pulling at the tangles, and applied fresh make-up. At last she told him, "I'm ready."

He put the magazine aside and looked her over without comment. As they drove back to the office he said, "Send those mud-stained clothes to the cleaners and charge it to the firm. After all, it happened in the course of your work."

"Thanks. All the same, it was my fault for wandering away."

"In search of the past?"

"Perhaps."

"I can't understand why you don't let the past rest in peace."

"Don't worry, I'm going to. From this moment on, for me the past is dead."

"And history will never be allowed to repeat itself?"

"Never." After a pause she asked, "Are those notes I took very important, Dirk?"

"Yes, they are. I shall have a number of copies printed and at the next site meeting I'll go through them with the builders, making sure the problems raised in them have been tackled. All instructions have to be issued in writing, because they affect the cost of the work. Everything that happens on the site is priced and added up, and then the quantity surveyor (Neville, for instance) checks it for me and also for our clients. As the building goes up, the number of sub-contractors gets bigger and everything becomes much more complex. The architect has to answer a lot of questions and has to make a great many quick decisions."

"I didn't realise before how complicated an architect's work is. And," she looked at him as if offering an apology for her lack of sympathy and understanding in the past, "how it requires total dedication."

"It's a pity, isn't it," he remarked in an odd tone, "that your realisation has come over three years too late?"

As soon as Marisa saw the flat, she decided to accept the tenancy. The house was old, the decorations in need of attention and the bedroom which had been converted into a kitchen was small and claustrophobic, but she was used to such drawbacks, having been conditioned to them by her experiences in the past.

The furniture was shabby but reasonably comfortable. There was a draw-leaf dining table, a sideboard with loose handles and a wall cupboard with glass sliding doors. The carpet, which did not quite fit, had obviously been bought in a sale. The bedroom had rugs over the brown-stained wooden floor. There was a double bed, and it had probably been purchased with a married couple in mind.

"At least it would be somewhere to live," Elwyn commented. "And the rent is reasonable. You'll need your own bed linen, though, and towels and so on."

They left the flat and Elwyn said he would ring the landlady to let her know Marisa had decided to take the accommodation. He used the telephone in the hotel entrance foyer and afterwards told Marisa that everything had been settled.

As she sat with Elwyn in the hotel dining-room, she sensed a change coming over him. It was a kind of metamorphosis, like a caterpillar into a butterfly, from humble shop assistant to imperious plutocrat commanding the deferential waiter to do his bidding. It was almost as if, without even being aware of it, he was acting on a stage in front of an audience. It was a part that was new to him, therefore difficult to sustain, but sustain it he must, until the show was over.

With a tinge of hauteur, he gave the order and when the waiter departed, Elwyn gave a self-satisfied smile as if congratulating himself on carrying the part off with such conviction. To Marisa, who knew him so well, it was a little pathetic and even amusing, but she played up to him as if she were the leading lady supporting him in his difficult role.

But when the wine waiter, as formidably knowledgeable about

wines as the aristocracy itself, presented him with the wine list, his carefully nurtured suavity crumbled like a piece of cake in a baby's hand. He looked the list over uncertainly and without consulting Marisa, handed it back, waving it away with a sheepish shake of the head. But apart from that momentary lapse, he carried through his slightly haughty, falsely confident air to the end of the meal.

Marisa suggested that they should sit in the lounge, where they could talk, but Elwyn said,

"What about your room? I haven't seen it yet. You remember last time I came Dirk was here."

Marisa could see no reason why she should not take Elwyn up to her room. She knew him well enough to have no fears about his behaviour.

But for once she was wrong. There was a side to him she did not know at all. There must have been something about the exclusive atmosphere of the hotel which had gone to his head. He wandered about the bedroom, soaking up the semi-luxury, his personality almost visibly expanding beyond its normal narrow limits. He switched on the light over the mirror above the wash basin, smoothed back his straw-coloured hair and straightened his tie. It seemed that he was beginning to feel quite at home, as if all this luxuriant comfort was his due, as if he was at last, in his own opinion, in his true environment.

He confronted Marisa and there was a decidedly amorous look in his eyes. He did not say anything, just stood in front of her as she closed the wardrobe door, having put her coat away. Then he clasped her shoulders and pulled her towards him.

He placed a kiss on her lips and stood back, as if estimating the effect of it on her. Her main reaction was one of surprise. Since she did not push him away he repeated the experiment, then his arms came round her awkwardly and with a show of manly strength he urged her towards the bed.

When she realised what he was doing, she said, "No, Elwyn, no. Don't be silly!"

"I'm not being silly." He impelled her downwards until they were half-reclining side by side.

"I can't – I'm not –"

He tried to kiss her again, and to her dismay her resistance only seemed to strengthen his determination. This was a new Elwyn, one she had never dreamed existed and one she found quite distasteful. She pulled away and as he struggled with her there was an element of desperation in his advances, as if he were thinking that she must not be allowed to frustrate his masculinity now it had fought against enormous odds to break through to the surface.

But his hopes and the liberation of his personality from its habitual restraints were doomed, like the life-span of a butterfly, to be short-lived. There was a knock on the door and Marisa gazed at Elwyn with dismay. It wasn't – it couldn't be Dirk! She pulled away and tried to smooth her hair, but it was too untidy to do much about it. Its disorder would tell the caller all he – or she – would want to know.

The knock came again and this time she hurried to open the door – it might be one of the hotel staff. As Elwyn saw Dirk enter, he turned a bright, guilty scarlet. Dirk looked from him to Marisa, noting her confusion, and he said, his voice heavy with sarcasm,

"Don't tell me I've come at the wrong moment?"

The part Elwyn had written for himself in the play of the evening rose to impassioned, resentful heights. Frustrated desire inflamed him into a self-righteous rage. He, Elwyn Worrell, was still the imperious domineering plutocrat. This man who had strolled so nonchalantly on to the stage had no right to be there. There was no part in the play for him. He must be got rid of with all possible speed before he stole the show from the leading man.

Elwyn stood up. "Look here, old chap," he said, his voice pinched and throaty, his eyes staring with anger, "you've no right to come barging in here, interfering in Marisa's private life."

If he had really meant to rid the stage of the unwanted character, then he had definitely chosen the wrong thing to say. The unwanted character took over the leading role with such effect that Elwyn Worrell became a player so subordinate to the plot as to grow practically redundant. The roles were completely reversed.

Dirk narrowed his eyes and said through his teeth, *"Right,* did you say? I've got as much damned *right* in this room as any husband has in his wife's bedroom. We're not divorced yet, and until we are, I've got the right – the legal right – to do whatever I like with her and to her – within reasonable limits – either with or without her consent. I also have the *right* to ask you to leave. I could, if I liked, throw you out. But I'm being gentlemanly – with the greatest reluctance – and merely asking you to go."

Elwyn collapsed on to the bed and the transition began to take place in the reverse order. He was once again the servile, humble shop assistant. The play was over. It had been a fiasco.

"My restraint," Dirk continued, standing over him, "is all the more remarkable because it was you who in the first place broke up our marriage." Elwyn began to protest, but did not get any further than opening his mouth. "You," Dirk went on, "were the perpetual irritant, the ineradicable factor which pestered and worried and interfered with our married lives to such an extent that you made our life together impossible." He looked at Marisa. "I don't suppose my wife has told you – she's no doubt maintained a tight-lipped silence – about our constant and unremitting rows over you."

"But," Elwyn spluttered, "I didn't break up your marriage. You did. You walked out on her."

Dirk said to Marisa, "Tell him why."

"Dirk, please –"

"Because," he ignored her plea, "of you, and only you. So I repeat – get out!"

"I'm going with him," Marisa cried. "You can't turn him out of my room like that!" She could not tell him that it was not so much that she wanted to go with Elwyn as to escape from what he, Dirk, might say or do to her if she stayed.

"Your room?" Dirk demanded. "Who' paying?"

"Yes, that's something you *would* hold over me, isn't it? Elwyn's been good to me in so many ways I –" Her fear of Dirk getting the better of her, she seized her coat from the wardrobe and ran to join Elwyn at the door, but Dirk's hand came out, clamped viciously round her arm and jerked her back.

"You're staying here."

"You can't make me –"

"Can't I?" He gripped both her arms and pulled them behind her, grasping her wrists as tightly as if his hands were a pair of handcuffs. He was hurting and her tears welled up.

Elwyn left, closing the door behind him. Dirk let her go.

"So I came at the wrong time, did I? I spoilt the great love scene."

She sank on to the bed, holding her head, knowing that even if she told him the truth he would not believe her.

"By heaven," he said, walking about the room, "he's been asking for that. For years it's been like an open wound with me. Now I've got it off my chest, now I've told him just what he did to us, perhaps the wound will heal. It may leave a scar, but a little plastic surgery will put that right." He smiled maliciously. "The plastic surgery of the love of a woman – another woman."

He stood in front of her huddled form and she mumbled, "Why did you come?" She took away her hands and stared up at him. "This is the second time you've come here knowing I'd have someone with me. First Greg, now Elwyn. I wish you'd stop interfering. We are separated, as you take delight in reminding me. You seem to forget how good Elwyn's been, helping me over difficult times –"

"*Good* to you? In prising me from you, in pushing me out of your life? You call that being 'good'? My word, I didn't realise until now what an ill-matched couple we were. So you want me to stop interfering, as you put it? All right, I'll go. But don't come running to me when you're in trouble. From now on I'm just another man, joined to you in no other way except, for the time being and until you marry again, in name." He went to the door and opened it.

Afraid of the resolution in his voice and that he really meant what he was saying, she ran after him. "Dirk! Don't go. I mean, why did you *really* come?" She knew her words were a form of apology, a retraction of the accusation she had made that he had come only to interfere. He must have accepted it as the apology she had intended because he moved back into the room and closed the door.

"That's better," he said. "I'm glad you realised in time I meant what I said. I came to ask if you needed any furniture for your flat and if so, to tell you I would go with you to the repository and arrange to have some of the stuff moved for you."

"That – was kind of you. Thank you for being so thoughtful."

"So I've got some virtues? You astonish me! Well, will you need anything for the flat?"

"Yes, I will. It's furnished, but I shall have to provide my own bed linen and so on. And the bedside and coffee tables would be useful. I'd also like the record player and a chair or two."

"I'll phone the removal firm and fix a time for us to go there. I believe they need notice so that they can move other people's property to let us get at our things."

"Our things," he had said. She looked at him, searchingly, hopefully, but his face was as empty as a beach in midwinter, without a single reminder of summer days gone by.

He moved to go and she said, "Dirk?"

He stood still, raising his eyebrows. "Well?"

"Thank you for all you've done, for paying for this room and for increasing my allowance and – for being so good to me in other ways." Somehow she couldn't meet his eyes. "I just – didn't want you to think it's all been unappreciated."

He came back to her. "So I'm 'good' to you, am I? Thanks for telling me. But there's one thing you'll do over my dead body – and that is classify me with your wonderful friend Elwyn Worrell, who's also been so 'good' to you. A friend is something I'll never be to you, my dear wife, until – and even after – the divorce court us do part."

CHAPTER VII

When Dirk called Marisa to his room next day to take dictation, she reminded him of the rehearsal that evening.

"I hadn't forgotten," he said tersely. "I shall be behind the stage making a start on the scenery. There may be some noise – hammering, sawing and so on. I hope it won't disturb the cast."

She said they would just have to get used to it.

"I rang the repository," he told her, "and we can go there any time in the next few days. When are you planning to move?"

"As soon as possible. I've warned the hotel I'll be leaving any day, probably this coming weekend. I shall have the key of the flat by then."

"If you move in on Saturday, I can give you some help."

"Well, Elwyn did say –" The look in his eyes stopped her. "Thanks, I'd appreciate it."

He smiled down at the letter he was holding. He had scored a point.

"Would it be convenient for us to collect the stuff after work tomorrow?" she asked.

He nodded. "We can take it back to my place until you move in, if you like." He looked at her quickly, cynically. "Don't say it – 'Elwyn said I could leave it at his aunt's house'."

"Well, he did, but I'd rather leave it with you."

"You can't mean it! Your childlike trust touches me to the heart."

"It's not a matter of trust. It's just that –" She looked at him. "It used to be ours."

He frowned. "You came to work, so let's get on with it."

Dirk arrived at the rehearsal in a buoyant mood. He stripped off his suede car coat and flung it on a chair, revealing a blue, crew-necked pullover. His trousers, although he declared they were old, still looked good, probably because they had been expensive in the first place.

"Behold," he said to the others who had gathered round, "the architect, disciplined by his training to utilise to the full both his imagination and his intellect, not only willing – but able – to use his hands. And he doesn't mind dirtying them either." He looked round. "Norman? Come on, where are these flats we're going to work on? Got the tools and the paint? I've brought some with me, but I doubt if it will be enough for what I have in mind."

Sally's face appeared on the stage in a gap between the closed curtains. She spotted Dirk, flung the curtains apart, raced down the wooden steps and threw herself across the hall.

"Dirk!" She stood panting in front of him, gazing up into his face.

"Hallo," he said, smiling, "what are you after? As if I didn't know!"

She grinned. "A kiss, like the one you gave me before."

"My word, if ever a girl asked for it . . ." He obliged and she squealed when he released her. He flicked a spiteful glance at Marisa, who had been watching the incident like an unsuccessful entrant in a beauty contest being forced to witness the crowning of the winner.

Then he said, "I don't know what my girl-friend would think if she saw me kissing another woman like that."

Sally pouted. "You haven't got a girl-friend, have you?"

"I have. She's a rich widow and I'm designing a house for her."

"Are you going to live in it with her?"

"I might, young Sally. You never know."

"No, no," Sally cried, "you can't do that!"

Marisa turned away feeling like a ventriloquist with Sally acting as the 'dummy' – the words she had just used might have come from Marisa's own mouth.

"Can't I?" Dirk answered Sally. "Who's to stop me?"

"Me," said Sally, winding her arms round his neck. "I'll be your girl-friend."

He laughed with the others and gently detached himself from her hold. "It doesn't do to *offer,* you know. You should let the

106

man do the chasing, don't you know, in the first instance at least."

Sally said sulkily, walking back towards the stage, "I don't need any lessons from you on how to get my man."

Everyone laughed, and Dirk muttered good-humouredly, *"You* are telling me!"

The rest of the cast followed the leading lady up the steps and on to the stage. Dirk said quietly to Marisa, "Where's your tame hero tonight? Deserted you for another woman?"

"As a matter of fact," she said icily, "he's got a sore throat and thought it best to stay away. One of the others is standing in for him."

Dirk called to Norman that he was going in search of work and they disappeared behind the scenes. Throughout the evening there was a background noise of intermittent sawing and hammering. At times the actors had to raise their voices to make themselves heard above it. But Marisa thought it prudent to say nothing to the two men who were causing the distraction. She guessed that Norman would be apologetic, but knew she would get a rude answer from the man he was assisting.

When the rehearsal was over, people drifted off. Sally went up to Dirk, hung on his arm and asked in a wheedling tone, "Will your girl-friend mind if you give me a lift home?"

He laughed. "Well, now," he pretended to think about it, "I wonder if she would." He looked round. "Marisa, what do you think? Will my girl-friend mind if I give Sally a lift?"

"You'd better phone her and ask permission," Marisa answered sourly. She dragged on her coat, wrapped her scarf tightly round her neck and pulled on her gloves, making for the door.

"Marisa?"

She turned back to Dirk.

"Have you got your car?"

"No. It's at the garage. There's something wrong with the gears."

"Care for a lift?"

"No, thanks." She turned her back to him. "You've already got yourself a passenger. You won't want me."

"Oh, but," his voice was soft, suggestive. "I do want you."

She swung round, her eyes angry, her heart throbbing. Only she knew what he meant. He was smiling.

Sally said petulantly, "You're taking *me* home, Dirk. You can't take two of us."

"There's no rule against it, young woman. I can take anyone I like home. I suppose you think you'll be done out of your goodnight kiss." He patted her hand. "Don't worry, I make a habit of dispensing goodnight kisses to all the women I take home." He moved his eyes. "So take warning, Marisa."

She went out, but he was after her at once, pulling Sally with him. He linked his arm in Marisa's and when she tried to pull away, his hand sought and grasped hers so that she couldn't escape.

"Can't you see she doesn't want to come?" said Sally.

"She's coming," Dirk said, so curtly Sally looked at him.

"Anyone would think," came the peevish voice in the darkness, "that Marisa was your girl-friend and not the rich widow."

Dirk laughed loudly. "You must be joking!"

He unlocked the car and Sally grabbed the front seat. Marisa climbed into the back and huddled in a corner. "You'll take her home first, won't you?" Sally asked, moving her head towards Marisa.

He smiled through the windscreen at the darkness ahead. "Since you're the younger, you should be in bed earlier, so I'll take you home first, Sally."

"Me, *young*? I'm eighteen. How can you call me young?"

He laughed, but said no more until he drew up outside her home. She leaned towards him and held out her lips. He held back, but it might have been only to tantalise her. "You promised, Dirk!"

"If any girl asked for trouble!" he muttered. He took her by the shoulders and kissed her. She wasn't satisfied and wanted another, but he got out, walked round to her side of the car and opened the door. "Come on, young woman. A man's not safe with you!"

Sally laughed, waved gaily to both of them and disappeared into the darkness. He drove on for a few minutes, then drew up again.

He said, over the noise of the engine, "I know you're sulking because Sally usurped your place in the front. So come on," he patted the seat beside him, "join me."

"No, thank you." Marisa's lips were as stiff as cardboard. "I'll stay where I am."

He switched off the engine and folded his arms. "We're staying here until you do as I say."

She knew by the obstinate set of his head that he meant it, so with reluctance she opened the door and walked round the front of the car, turning her head from the dazzle of the headlights, and got in beside him.

Instead of dropping her outside the hotel entrance, Dirk drove straight into the car park. She wondered why, but she did not have to wonder for long.

"Thanks for the lift." She started to open the door, but he stopped her.

"Just a minute, my *darling* wife. You know what I said to Sally – always a goodnight kiss."

"Don't be silly." She tried to escape from his hold. "You didn't mean it."

"Didn't I?" He adjusted the position of the driving seat, pushing it well clear of the steering wheel, took her by the shoulders and swung her round until she was lying in his arms. Then he kissed her with a passion which she knew was simulated and utterly false. She tried to pull away, but was trapped by his greater strength.

He lifted his lips from hers and whispered, "Does Elwyn kiss you like that? Do you cling to him as you're clinging to me, as though I were about to fall from a cliff top and you were holding me back?"

Before she could loosen her hold, he was kissing her again, stirring her so deeply this time that she began to respond. Half-remembered ecstasies cut a swathe of dazzling light across the surface of her mind like a winter sun shining brilliantly on a restless sea. She felt her ardour rise, lifting her to long-forgotten heights. He knew still how to arouse her, and she was allowing him to do so. And she was terrified — at what he was doing to her emotions and her will-power.

She struggled again and this time he freed her.

"Well?" he asked softly. "Is this the night? You ask me in and I stay? And afterwards you're free of me? You get the divorce you want so much?"

"No," she whispered hoarsely, "no, no to all your questions."

"So, we remain as we are for an indefinable length of time. You know my condition and until you fulfil it," he shrugged, "nothing changes. It's all the same to me. Goodnight, Marisa."

This time she got out of the car unmolested. But she bent down and tapped on the window. He reached across and opened it.

"What now?" He sounded angry, as if in that few seconds his control had snapped.

"Dirk, you promised to take me to the repository tomorrow."

"I hadn't forgotten. Now take your hand off my car and let me get home."

"Dirk ..." Her voice wavered. She wanted him, she ached for him, but she had to let him go. "I'm sorry."

"Are you?" He shot away into the darkness.

In the entrance hall after work next day, Marisa waited for Dirk. She looked anxiously up the sweep of the staircase wondering if he had forgotten after all, when she saw Greg coming down.

"Hi, beautiful. Waiting for me?"

"Sorry, no," she laughed.

He lingered, stroking his beard. "You wouldn't be free tonight? I've got an invitation to a party. So far, no partner."

Her eyes lifted again to watch Dirk coming down the stairs, pulling on his driving gloves. Greg was saying, "It's not a formal affair. Some friends are giving it, a married couple, so it'll be perfectly respectable." Dirk stood beside Marisa. Greg eyed him dubiously, but pressed on anyway, "Care to come with me?"

Now Marisa looked at Dirk. He seemed amused at the way they were both seeking his approval. "What's this?" he asked. "Inviting her to a party?" He looked at his wife. "Well, go on, don't disappoint the man. I give you my permission."

"Thanks, Greg," she answered, "but I'm not in a party mood. Sorry. Nice of you to ask me, though."

Greg left them.

"Now he's a disappointed man," Dirk mocked. "Why didn't you give him a consolation kiss, like the one you gave Elwyn? Do you make a habit of raising a man's hopes, only to dash them, then insult him by saying you're 'sorry'?"

"If you're referring to last night—"

"Let's forget last night," he snapped, opening the door for her to leave in front of him. "Where's your car?"

"At the hotel. I came by bus this morning. Incidentally, I can take the stuff straight to the flat. The landlady's given me permission."

He nodded and they were silent for the rest of the journey.

The repository was dark and soulless, like a mortuary for dead dreams. There was a dank, heavy smell as though the windows had not been opened for years. Pieces of furniture, crowded into groups in the vast warehouse, were once homes, had meaning, function, a place in life; They had been part of a family, familiar things grown dear down the years. Now they were abandoned, lost, stripped of significance and purpose, perhaps never again to fit into new places, new houses acquired by their owners.

Marisa and Dirk were led through the narrow alleyways between the carefully separated and labelled furniture, and left to themselves. It was not until she was confronted with the possessions which she and Dirk had once called their 'home' that she realised how pathetic it all was.

He stood back, letting her make her choice, as if he disowned the stuff. And it was his attitude of repudiation which hurt her most. It was as if he were rejecting the past — the past they

111

had shared. These possessions had not been theirs long enough to have acquired any meaning. They were as dead and dispensable as last year's calendar.

Marisa opened drawers, drew out bed linen, towels, clothes. Some of it, she saw with dismay, was already touched with mildew, as though it had not completely recovered from the soaking it had received the day she was evicted from her home. These she packed in boxes given her by the warehouse superintendent. She told Dirk the items of furniture she wanted and he said he thought he could get them into his car, either in the boot or the back seat.

As they left the dim, cold premises, she felt both relief and an infinite sadness. She had seen the past again, and she had been filled with such misery she wanted to cry. Their marriage was in that repository, too, and like so many of the things under that roof, abandoned, never to be claimed again by the owners.

"Where's this flat?" Dirk asked shortly.

She gave him the address and he turned into the drive of a large old house, which stood some way back from the main road. It had known better days, when the whole area had flourished and buzzed with middle-class life. Now the district was classified as bordering on the dubious, just and only just, respectable.

"Got the key?" She took it out of her bag and showed him. "Come on, then, let's take this stuff in. I'm in a hurry. I've got a date this evening."

She did not need to ask with whom – Luella, of course.

He volunteered the information, "It's Patrick's birthday, and he's having a party. I'm giving Luella a hand."

It was like having a bayonet driven into her body and twisted. She nearly screamed with pain. Luella's son, a party, family life such as she had never known.

When they had carried the last of the items upstairs, Dirk looked round. The architect in him seemed to wince, like an artist being shown an appalling painting. "My God, you do choose some places to live in! I suppose the attraction is the nearness of beloved Elwyn." He wandered into the bedroom, tested the double bed, made a face when it sagged towards the middle. He went into the kitchen and tutted. "All mod. cons., as they say, except that 'modern' in this case means about a quarter of the way through the century."

"What difference does it make to me?" Marisa asked hopelessly. "This sort of thing is all I've been used to. Even as a child I never knew what it was like to have a proper home, bright, cheerful, modern," she caught his eye, "architect-designed." She turned away, shoulders drooping. "Never will."

"Why not? You'll have to get Elwyn to provide you with one."

She could not stand his sarcasm. She flopped down into an armchair. Dirk looked at his watch. "I must be off. Come on, I'll give you a lift to the hotel."

Marisa rested her head against the upholstery and turned her face away. "No, thanks. I'll go back by bus. You go to your party – and your girl-friend." With a grim smile, she repeated the words he had used earlier. "I give you my permission." The smile faded and her lips trembled.

There was a short silence. "Please yourself," he said at last, and went.

It was just as well he left when he did, Marisa thought, because if he had stayed a few moments longer, he would have seen the tears pouring down her cheeks.

That weekend Marisa left the hotel and moved into her flat. It was unheated and smelled of damp, having been empty for some weeks. She switched on the two electric fires she had brought from the repository, but it took them a long time to take the chill off the air.

Elwyn came later and helped her settle in. She cooked a meal and they ate it in the dining-room. The flat possessed an old television set and Elwyn retuned it for her. They watched for a while and before he left she made some coffee.

She wanted an early night, she told him. Moving in had proved something of an upheaval. She hoped he wouldn't be difficult as he had been at the hotel, but apparently there was

113

nothing in that unexciting, commonplace atmosphere to go to his head. He behaved circumspectly and gave her a brief but affectionate kiss before he left.

On Monday morning, Dirk caught her as she was going to Mr. Garner's office. He asked how she liked her new home.

"At least it's my own. Elwyn helped me settle in."

"Yes, I thought he would. That's why I didn't offer. I would have hated to be in the way." He shut himself and his sarcasm in his room.

A few days later, before the other typists arrived, Jan reminded Marisa about the firm's annual dinner. A collection had been made some time before for a leaving present for Mr. Hilsby. "Taking Elwyn?" Jan asked.

Marisa nodded. "Jan, who's going with Dirk?"

"According to what he told Neville, Luella. Marisa," her manner became confidential, "just how involved is Dirk getting with that woman?"

"How should I know? From the sound of it, they're bosom friends. He's already acting the part of the little boy's step-father."

"Does it worry you, dear?" The sympathy behind the words was almost Marisa's undoing, but she controlled her voice as she answered,

"Even if it did, what good would it do? One day we'll get a divorce, and he'll marry his rich widow. But there's nothing really to keep them apart now, is there? They're both mature people, they can be discreet, they could even live together if they wanted . . ." Her voice broke and she turned away.

Jan's arm went round her shoulders. "Don't break your heart over him, love. No man's worth it."

With great strength of mind, Marisa held back the tears. "Thanks for sympathising, Jan." She smiled weakly. "Don't know what I'd do without you."

Jan patted her shoulder as the other girls trooped in, laughing and talking.

A few days before the firm's annual dinner, Marisa went shopping for a new party dress. Jan insisted on going along with her.

"We're getting something stunning. We're searching for a new image – the new 'you'. Somehow we've got to restore your confidence. We shall have to do some architectural planning on you and design a new Marisa Sterling. Something that'll make husband Dirk sit up and beg!"

Marisa laughed. "I can't image Dirk begging for anything, especially for a woman. He doesn't have to – they all go running to him." She told Jan about Sally. "Every time she sees Dirk she practically throws herself at him!"

Together they toured the department stores and at last found a dress to please Jan. But to Marisa, although Jan enthused, it was so out of character she wanted to reject it. The dress was black and high-waisted, its bodice glittering with silver thread, the sleeves were wrist-length and the neckline plunged daringly low. The plain skirt touched her ankles, flaring a little towards the hem.

"A jet necklace to emphasise your fair skin plus long matching earrings – and you'll be a work of art." Jan stood back to admire her as if the girl in front of the mirror were her own creation.

"It's no good, Jan, I can't wear it."

"You must, Marisa. In fact, if you don't buy it, I'll pay for it and make you a present of it, then you'll have to wear it."

In the end Marisa bought it. When Elwyn called for her to take her to the dinner, he gaped. "My goodness, Marisa," he got out, "you look great!"

"I don't feel great." She put on her coat, wrapping it round her as if by doing so she could exorcise the dress whose potential capacity for attracting attention was already haunting her like a ghost.

The hotel, built in the style of a country club, seemed to be swarming with guests. There were people Marisa had never seen before, strange faces that stared through her, dismissing her as just another employee. Here and there she saw people from the office, and at these she smiled, desperate to form a link with someone who was familiar in that milling, laughing alien crowd.

She left Elwyn and pushed her way into the ladies' cloakroom to comb her hair and renew her make-up. She adjusted the long black earrings which swung from her ears, delaying parting with her coat until the last moment. When at last she took it off and handed it to the attendant, she felt like a deep-sea diver plunging in without his life-preserving equipment. The other women, typists, tracers, wives and friends of the many architects, surveyors and technical staff who had come from the firm's other branches, hardly spared her a glance. They were too engrossed in their own appearance to bother about her. Jan rushed in, stopped short at the sight of Marisa, drew a breath and let it out as a whistle.

"That should do the trick!"

"I feel terrible, Jan. I wish I'd brought a cardigan!"

"A cardigan over that dynamite? You must be mad, love. You'll outshine our dear Luella, that's for certain."

"Hurry, Jan," Marisa urged. "I don't want to go out there alone."

"Oh, you go, love. I'll be hours fixing my make-up. Neville rushed me so much at home I had to leave off my mascara and eye-shadow." Still Marisa lingered. "Elwyn will be waiting for you, won't he? Go on, Marisa," Jan pleaded, "don't you start hurrying me now!"

So Marisa left the sanctuary of the cloakroom and found Elwyn standing alone and uncertain, his eyes seeking for her as eagerly as hers were searching for him. She joined him, turning her back on the crowd and smiling at her partner.

"It's not," a voice said behind her, "our Marisa?"

She turned to face Greg, regarding him as a test case. He gazed at the picture she presented like a connoisseur at an art exhibition. His eyes revealed that he had uncovered a hitherto unknown masterpiece, certain to be established by the experts as the genuine article. This, his eyes said, was the real thing, the true Marisa Sterling.

"My, my!" came at last from lips he seemed to be licking like a ravenous wolf. "Who was the architect who designed and created you? I'll bet it wasn't your ever-loving husband. Is he

116

here yet?" He looked about him. "I must – but must – witness the impact."

"Run away, Greg," Marisa urged, embarrassed now. "I feel conspicuous enough without you making things worse."

"Don't be so self-conscious, beautiful. Turn round, give the boys a treat."

Guests were moving into the next room where before-dinner drinks were being served. Greg went on ahead followed by Marisa at Elwyn's side. As they entered, heads turned. This time those strangers did not look through her, or dismiss her as a nonentity. Their eyes lingered and asked 'Who is she?'

Jan, passing with Neville, whispered, "I told you you were dynamite, dear."

Neville waved, looked and gazed. He said to his wife a little breathily, "Where did that vision come from?"

Jan reached round and patted herself on the back. "All my own work, Neville."

"I might have known," he said with amused affection. To Marisa, ingenuously, "Seen Dirk yet?"

"I don't think he's arrived, Neville."

"He has. I saw him come in with that woman client of his." He looked at the door. "Ah, here they are."

Luella entered first, cool and beautiful in red and white. Her skirt, scarlet and classically straight, touched the floor, and the long-sleeved top was made from ruffled white lace. Her fair hair was dressed high and topped with a hairpiece. Her looks were imperious and cold.

"There, darling," whispered Neville to his wife, "is the answer to your question as to how far Dirk's progressed in his relations with her. Any man who got too near her would be turned to ice with her."

Marisa, afraid to meet her husband's eyes, sought refuge in conversation. "Neville," she said urgently, "tell me who's here. There are so many strange faces –"

"There are a lot I don't know myself, Marisa." He raised his head and looked over the crowd. "I can see Mr. Garner and his wife and there's Mr. Hilsby and his wife. Greg's over there watching you like a fox in search of a vixen. His companions have you under close observation, too." He moved back. "Dirk! Good to see you."

Now her husband was there and Marisa was forced to look at him. His eyes, as he appraised her, were withdrawn and assessing. So Jan had been mistaken. Dirk was not only unimpressed, he was coldly critical.

Luella, beside him, had assumed an interested, party smile, looking at her companion's friends and colleagues as if waiting to be acknowledged as one of them and admitted to their closed circle. Jan and Neville were polite and friendly, allowing her, as it were, a foot in the door. But no more.

"This, Luella," Dirk was saying, "is Marisa, my wife. My estranged wife." The emphasis on the penultimate word was deliberate and unmistakable.

The cool eyes of his woman friend were momentarily heated by a glow of warmth which was as effective as a half-kilowatt electric fire in a banqueting hall. The head was inclined with the majesty of a royal personage, the hand extended with as much enthusiasm as a visitor to a zoo putting her hand through the bars of a tiger's cage.

Marisa was stunned that Dirk, the ardent, passionate man she had known in the early days of her marriage, could have become so devoid of feelings since they had parted that he could even contemplate any form of liaison, either legal or illegal, between himself and this frigid creature. Involuntarily she turned puzzled, questioning eyes towards him, only to feel them rebound, like a ship colliding with an iceberg, from the rebuke in his.

Jan whispered to her husband. He nodded and murmured to Luella, "Come with me, Mrs. Ackland, and I'll find you a drink. Look, here's the man of the evening, Mr. Hilsby, one of the principals of the firm. He's retiring, you know ..." With tact, firm and persuasive, he led her away.

Jan seized Elwyn. "Come on," she said, "I'm not going to be left without a man. Get me a drink, there's a dear." With a long, meaningful look at Marisa, she led the reluctant Elwyn away.

So, by a clever manoeuvre, Marisa and Dirk were left alone. For a time they did not speak. He leaned against the great empty wood-carved fireplace, and let his eyes feel their way over her. There was no praise in them, nor admiration.

"What are you after," he said softly, "wearing a dress like that?" He held up his hand. "Don't tell me, I can guess. You really must be desperate."

She held herself in, refusing to be baited.

"You should put a 'For Sale' notice round your neck in place of that necklace," his eyes lowered insultingly, "plus the words 'reduction for quantity.' Then you would get more offers from the men in the party than you could cope with."

"If you're implying that this dress was cheap, you're wrong. It was quite expensive."

"My dear woman, I wasn't implying that the *dress* was cheap."

"Look, Dirk," she was near to tears, the little self-confidence she had gained slipping away from her fast, "I know you don't like me, but is there any need to be so insulting?"

"Am I insulting you? If so, I'm sorry, but you really are asking for trouble, and my word, if I weren't under an obligation to partner the woman I've brought with me, you'd get it before the night was out." He glanced round. "Oddly enough, I'm the only man here with the legal right to give you the 'trouble' you're asking for." He saw her mounting anger. "What's the matter? Are you itching to slap my face? I warn you, if you do, I'll slap back – harder."

She swung round and left him, searching for Jan. It looked as though Jan had been watching them, and as Marisa approached, she said, "Is he at it again, love? I hope you gave as good as you got."

Marisa shook her head, unable to say a word. Jan nudged Neville, who thrust a drink into Marisa's hand. They watched Dirk stroll across to join Luella, who was talking to Greg. Somehow he had made her laugh, and Luella told the joke to Dirk, who laughed with them.

The guests were drifting into the dining-room and looking

for their names. Elwyn joined Marisa and were surprised to find that they had been placed near the top table. Dirk, of course, was with the other principals of the firm at the top table itself. By his side sat Luella, every inch the lady, fitting perfectly into the mould of the companion of one of the firm's top men.

Mr. Hilsby, as he took his place, saw Marisa and lifted his hand in a warm greeting. She smiled back. Mr. Garner nodded his smile brief but pleasant. Jan and Neville, to Marisa's relief were placed opposite herself and Elwyn. The meal progressed with laughter and chatter, efficiency and speed.

The time for the speeches and the toasts had come. Mr. Garner, with his usual brevity, gave an outline of Leonard Hilsby's career, the invaluable work he had done, his enthusiasm which had fired all who had come into contact with him. He announced with regret but understanding Mr. Hilsby's decision to retire, and presented the gift to which the entire firm had contributed. It was a movie camera, projector and screen, and three of the firm's youngest members had been chosen to present them.

Mr. Hilsby stood and accepted the gifts, then he fixed his spectacles firmly into position and surveyed his audience. First he thanked them sincerely for what they had given him, saying that in the extra leisure time he would now have at his disposal he would be able to indulge his hobby of moving photography more fully than ever before.

He went on, referring to his impending retirement, "The time has come for architecture and myself to go our separate ways. We don't see eye to eye any more." There was a ripple of amusement from the audience. "As I have so often told my inestimable secretary," he nodded towards Marisa and every eye was turned to her, "who has over the years worked for me intelligently and listened to me so patiently," Marisa stole a glance at Dirk, but he was staring straight ahead with an expression as blank as an empty picture frame, "I'm getting beyond it. I'm bewildered by the present and horrified by the future.

"When I read," he went on, "as I have done in my architectural journals, that architects are experimenting with pneumatic structures, making everything inflatable and disposable – walls, floors, furniture, you name it, they inflate it – I knew it was time for me to go. Easy to carry, they say, quick to put up, and quicker to throw away! And like fashions in clothes, they can be changed or abandoned as the situation demands."

He shook his head sadly. "And one day, they tell me, there will be all-plastic houses, plug-in cities, clip-on rooms, instant towns, concealed – even underground – architecture, all disposable, mobile, expendable." He scratched his head. "I don't know, they'll be inventing collapsible, chuckawayable people next!" There was a burst of laughter.

He looked down at his wife, white-haired, smiling, a tolerant, comfortable personality. "My wife, for instance – if ever there was an uncollapsible, unthrowawayable person, she's one." He paused for the laughter. "We've been married a good many years now, so many I've lost count. But, you see," he looked round, "there's a case in point. Nowadays we have disposable, deflatable, expendable marriages." More laughter. "It's true, you know. Marriage is not meant to last these days. It has 'built-in obsolescence', like cars some countries manufacture. This is the age of the 'throw-away' – clothes, furniture, morals, marriages. Couples stay together a year or two, then they're off in opposite directions."

Marisa's eyes were drawn across the room to Dirk. Had she hoped he would find a message there? But he looked back at her, his eyes as empty as a theatre after the last member of the audience had gone.

Mr. Hilsby sighed. "These young people, they don't know what they're missing, do they, my dear?" His wife looked up at him fondly. "They'll never know that, as a marriage gets older it develops meaning, solidity, a beauty all its own, like an intelligently planned, brilliantly conceived architectural masterpiece, acquiring character with the passage of the years, mellowing it, maturing it, as shadows and sunlight pass across its surfaces." He looked down at his wife, seriously this time. "We've had our troubles, our differences, but they all passed. The foundations were so well laid, they endured. We were never

121

tempted to tear up the original plan – our marriage certificate – as architects in the process of creating new designs tear up their original ideas."

There was a poignant silence. Marisa looked down at her hands, biting her lip.

"I seem to have strayed a little from the subject of my talk, myself and architecture. Yet I don't think so. Inflatable, disposable buildings are only temporary structures, not meant to last. Nor do temporary structures have baby temporary structures, so they don't need firm foundations." There was laughter at this. "But two young people coming together are by that very act forming the foundation for the future – the family. And that *is* meant to last." He paused. "Well, I may be retiring, but there's one thing I'll never retire from – marriage, to my wife, the only wife I've had and ever really wanted!"

The applause was long and sincere. Jan and Neville gazed into each other's eyes and Marisa saw their happiness with an unendurable envy. She looked across at her husband, but he was looking at Luella, who was looking at him. Any hope Marisa might have had that Mr. Hilsby's message had acted as a catalyst and changed and softened Dirk's attitude towards her toppled and crashed like rubble from a demolished building.

Soon afterwards the dinner ended. The guests left their seats and conversation became general. Somehow Marisa found herself separated from Elwyn, and even Jan and Neville had disappeared. She felt lost, bereft, like a child parted from its mother in the crush of customers in a department store.

"Hi there!" Greg pushed his way to her side. Following him were half a dozen young men, all of whom he introduced as his 'friends and colleagues from the Midlands branch of the firm.'

"They've been howling like wild dogs to meet you the whole evening," Greg said. "They all wanted a close-up view of the 'lady in black' as they called you. They also wanted to know who you were. I didn't tell them. I said you were the 'mystery woman'." He looked round at his friends. "This is Marisa, secretary to the top men of the firm." He introduced them and they crowded round her, trying to elbow each other out of the way.

"I've got a nice line in sports cars," one of the young men said. "Any time you'd like to try it out ..."

"I've got a nice line in etchings," said another. "Come and see them some time!"

"You wouldn't like to be my secretary, would you?" asked a third.

Marisa laughed at their questions and Greg, putting both his arms round her, said, "Get away, you lot. This girl's not on offer. She's —"

"If you pack of wolves would let me get at my wife," said a voice edged like the blade of a saw. They parted to let Dirk through and Greg's arms fell away from her.

"Your what?" asked one of the men. "Did you say your *wife*?"

Greg held up her left hand and they saw her wedding ring.

"But, Dirk," another said, "when you were down in the Midlands you told us you were separated from your wife."

"Quite right," replied Dirk. "We are separated."

"Good grief, Dirk, what's the matter with you? A girl like that —?"

"Lost your touch, Dirk?" taunted another. "Forgotten how to keep a woman happy?"

"Man," said one of the others, "if she were *my* wife, I wouldn't be able to keep my hands to myself!"

Dirk took Marisa's wrist between savage fingers, pulling her after him. "I want to introduce you to Mr. Markham, one of the principals at the Midlands branch," he looked back over his shoulder, "where those baying hounds have come from."

Marisa resisted. "Shouldn't you be introducing Luella to him? Why me? I don't matter to you any more."

"I'm not married to Luella — yet," he snapped.

She tried to get away. "All right, introduce her as your future wife."

"Will you be quiet?"

"No, I won't. I must get back to Elwyn." His fingers tightened, bruising her flesh. "You're hurting me, Dirk," she whispered tearfully.

"Good," he said, tightening his hold still more.

She bit her lip to stop herself protesting again. When they found the man they were seeking, Dirk's hand slid down from her wrist to her hand. She was so relieved to be freed from the relentless pressure of his fingers, she allowed him to hold it without protest.

"Mr. Markham." The man Dirk was addressing turned. He was tall, broad and grey-haired, his manner jovial, his smile warm. Dirk said, "May I introduce my wife, Marisa?"

"Ah, Mrs. Sterling." A large hand gripped hers. "I've been wanting to meet you. Your husband used to speak of you when he worked with us, before he left to return north and slip into Mr. Hilsby's shoes – or should I say seat?"

His laugh rang out and they laughed with him. He saw their linked hands and beamed, "Good to see you together again. Let's hope you've taken what Mr. Hilsby said to heart. It's true, you know, about marriage improving with the years. You ask any of us old 'uns!"

Marisa looked enquiringly at Dirk, but his face gave nothing away. She had not the heart to disillusion this pleasant man. She couldn't tell him, 'This is all a pretence, put on for the benefit of Dirk's image within the firm now he's one of its principals.'

Dirk chatted to Mr. Markham for a few minutes, then led her away.

She snatched her hand from his. "You've acted out that little charade, so you can go back to your girl-friend. She'd hate to see you walking hand-in-hand with your estranged wife. She might even throw you over, and that would never do, would it?" She ignored his anger which was coming to the boil like a steaming kettle. "Think of the fortune you'd forfeit if you lost your precious client."

"If I had my way," he said between his teeth, "I'd make you eat those words," his eyes plunged downwards with her neckline, "even if I had to force them down your beautiful throat!"

"Well, you won't have your way," she answered back, her eyes glittering in the splintered light from the chandeliers above

124

them, "and you can keep your compliments, insincere though they are, for your *beautiful* lady friend! I'm going to find Elwyn. I don't intend to desert him as you deserted me three years ago."

She thrust her way through the dispersing crowd and tried to forget the look on Dirk's face which, in her agony of mind, she interpreted as hatred.

CHAPTER VIII

THE play was progressing well. The date fixed for its presentation was approaching fast. During rehearsals, Dirk worked behind the scenes with Norman.

One lunchtime Dirk left his colleagues and strolled across to join Marisa and Jan who said, smiling, "Still lowering yourself to our level, Dirk? I should have thought that now you're one of the top men you'd have taken yourself off for lunch to one of the high class hotels, like Mr. Garner. How long are you going to go on mixing with the mob?"

Dirk pulled out the seat next to Marisa and sat down. "For as long as the mob tolerates me. When they start whispering behind their hands and freezing me out, I'll know it's time to go." He smiled at Marisa. "Go on, say it. I'm too democratic to be true."

She looked away uncomfortably. "Knowing what I do of you, I wouldn't have expected otherwise. You may have your faults, but snobbery isn't one of them."

"My word," he pretended to suffer from symptoms of shock and loosened his tie for a moment, "such compliments from you overwhelm me – muted though they are by unflattering qualifications about my 'faults'. You're not exactly free of them yourself."

Jan rubbed her hands. "Am I going to witness a marital argument? Carry on, you two, I'm all ears."

" 'Marital' is the wrong word, Jan," Dirk remarked coolly. "It doesn't apply to us any more."

"You disappoint me," she answered, rising briskly to join her husband. "I really thought for a moment that you were going to behave like a normal married couple, have a row, then effect a passionate reconciliation." Her voice grew oddly sharp. "Isn't it time you both stopped acting like idiots?"

They looked at her with some surprise, then at each other and

126

the silent question seemed to pass between them, 'What's biting her?' The wordless communication caught them unawares and was so unconscious and spontaneous, it was in itself almost sufficient to bring about the reconciliation Jan had so hopefully looked for.

"Are you free this evening?" Dirk asked, spinning an unused knife on the table top as though he were playing roulette.

Marisa smiled. "Are you asking me for a date?"

He smiled back. "I suppose in a way I am. The scenery's in a fit state to be seen by the producer without any danger of her wanting to fire the artist and creator on the spot. Tonight, can I pick you up and take you along to have a look at it? And, I hope, approve?"

"If you like."

The knife he was spinning kept stopping in one particular position and he seemed to be getting irritated with it.

"I won't ask you to a meal," she said. "You'd object to the slightly unpalatable concoctions I manage to turn out on my ancient cooker. Hardly the *haute cuisine* stuff you've grown used to."

He frowned and twirled the knife again. Still it stopped at the same place. Mechanically he straightened the cloth to see if it would have any effect. "I suppose Elwyn eats your 'concoctions', as you call them, as though they came from the kitchens of the Ritz!"

"He never complains."

He twirled the knife, furiously this time, so hard that it spun off the table. He cursed and bent down to pick it up. "Of course he wouldn't. Elwyn's perfect."

She said mildly, with the faintest of smiles, "He's no more perfect than you are."

Dirk scraped back his chair. His game of roulette was over. He had lost, hands down. "I'll call for you about eight." He returned to his colleagues.

It was snowing when Dirk called for her, not heavily, just a thin white curtain that settled lightly wherever it touched down – on the shoulders, the hair, the lips, melting to liquid when

127

the tongue reached out to draw the snowflakes in and test their neutral taste.

"I'm glad I'm not driving," Marissa commented, crossing her booted legs in the front seat and snuggling into the collar of her coat. "These conditions terrify me. I'm always scared of skidding."

"There are rules for getting yourself out of a skid. It's important that you should know how to cope with one. I'll have to take you through the motions some time. But you'd have to place your complete trust in me. Would you be able to do that?" She stayed silent. "Marisa?"

It took her some moments to give him an answer. "There was a time," she spoke slowly, "when I would have trusted you with my life."

He did not press the point. He didn't have to. She had given him his answer, by speaking in the past tense.

Norman was waiting for them at the hall.

"Stay here Marisa," Dirk instructed, "while Norman and I shift the scenery. We'll close the curtains so as to give you an audience's impression of the setting when they're opened."

They were gone for some time. She heard noises, laughter and an occasional curse when someone's foot or leg were hurt. "Over to you," Dirk said.

"Your way, Dirk," Norman called, "not too far, though."

"Ready?" came Dirk's voice from the stage. "Madam Producer, here we come."

The curtains drew apart and the set they had assembled related to the second act. There was a door to the left, the window in the centre, behind which was the 'view' so vital to the action. The french windows even had realistic-looking shutters, a touch Marisa had not expected. "The *chaise-longue* goes there," Norman said, pointing, "and the mirror will hang over the fireplace."

"Like it?" asked Dirk, coming to stand beside her.

Her shining eyes told him of her pleasure before she spoke. "Wonderful!" She looked at them both. "How can I thank you?"

Norman pointed. "Thank him. I just did what I was told. He had the ideas. He could almost be classed as a professional, do you know that?" To Dirk, "You could make a living at this sort of thing, mate, if you ever found yourself out of a job."

Dirk laughed. "If Garner, Sterling and Associates ever chuck me out, I won't need to worry, will I?"

Norman looked impressed. "You one of the top men? I didn't know that."

"I took Mr. Hilsby's place. Not quite drawing his salary yet, but according to Mr. Garner, it won't be long now. I certainly can't grumble at what I'm earning, though." He grinned at his wife. "Does that tempt you, Marisa, to come and live under my roof and share my earnings with me?"

"Hey, wait a minute, boy," Norman said, pretending to be alarmed, "are you proposing to her? Watch out, she might accept!"

Dirk laughed so loudly it echoed round the hall. Marisa walked towards the stage saying, "Money doesn't interest me that much. It doesn't guarantee married happiness."

"No? Perhaps not," Dirk said, "but it goes a hell of a long way towards it. Poverty and married happiness don't go well together, either." He caught her up. "Do they?"

She would not answer him. "Have you any more scenery to show me?"

Norman said, "Yes. Come on, Dirk, let's get the first act assembled. It may take some time, Marisa."

"Can I help?"

"No, thanks," said Norman.

"Yes, you can help," Dirk overruled him. "Three would be quicker than two."

"It's a bit much, isn't it," Norman commented, "expecting her to do any lifting?"

"She's not made of Dresden china," Dirk answered callously. "After all, she offered. If she hadn't meant it, she should have kept quiet. Come on, Marisa, behind the stage and take the weight with me."

Norman looked at her, expecting indignation, but was astonished to see her comply.

As Norman went to the other side of the piece of scenery, Dirk whispered in her ear, "Glad to know you've remembered rule one of a good marriage – all wives should be obedient to their husbands!" He dodged as she lifted her hand. "Now, now," he cautioned, still whispering, "If you go all Women's Lib on me, I'll soon put you back in your place – across my knee."

"If you don't stop annoying me," she whispered back fiercely, "I'll walk out!"

"That," he said aloud, "would be disastrous. Whoever heard of a producer walking out? Leading lady, yes, but producer, no."

"What's the matter, Marisa?" Norman asked. "Are you quarrelling with our artistic director? Don't do that, for heaven's sake. Humour him. He's too valuable to lose!"

"There you are, Mrs. Sterling," Dirk grinned, "you've had your orders – humour me." He murmured in her ear, "Later will do," then smiled at her murderous look.

Marisa gave her seal of approval to all the scenery they showed her. Before leaving, they stacked it away safely behind the scenes.

On the way back in Dirk's car, Marisa stared out of the window. She realised they were going in the wrong direction for her flat. "Where are you taking me?" she demanded.

"To my place. I thought you might make some coffee to warm us up. I knew if I'd asked you, you would have said 'no', so I didn't ask." He parked the car. "I also knew I wouldn't get an invitation to your place. Anyway, my flat's centrally heated. Yours resembles a refrigerator switched on to its coldest setting."

"I'm sorry you don't like my home, but it's really none of your business."

"Oh, stop arguing and come in."

Even when the heat of the flat welcomed them Marisa could not stop shivering. So Dirk turned on the imitation coal fire and she crouched in front of it. "Give me your coat," Dirk said, helping her take it off. "Now you can let the warmth get at you."

"I'll make some coffee."

130

"Stay where you are. I'll make it."

"There's no need to treat me like a guest. I'm only your wife — or rather, as you took delight in describing me to your lady friend, your 'estranged' wife."

He let the comment pass like an expert tennis player ignoring a ball hit out of court by his less-skilled opponent. While he made the coffee, Marisa huddled in front of the electric fire. She wondered why he had brought her back with him. She wondered how long she could stand their relationship drifting on in this oddly platonic fashion before she cracked under the strain. She could not go on for ever resisting the urge to touch him at will, to show her love for him in the way that any real wife could do. She looked into the future and the picture was so bleak she wanted to smash the crystal ball she had gazed into.

"Coffee, Marisa."

He was standing beside her. She straightened, took the cup he was offering her, and sat in an armchair. He sat, too.

"You know I'm going south to the Midlands for this three-day conference next week? Angela's coming with me, did you know?" She nodded. "I'm not too happy about it. I wish I were taking someone a little more mature. She's a nice girl, but not over-endowed with intelligence." He drank some coffee and glanced at her. "You — er — wouldn't come in her place, would you?"

Go with him as his secretary and not as his wife? Take second place, pretending there was nothing between them, not even friendship?

"Sorry, no."

He contemplated his drink, frowning. "That's what I thought you would say. It's a long time to be away from Elwyn, isn't it? Three whole days."

She did not contradict him. What was the use? she thought.

"As you know, I'm reading a paper to the conference on future trends in architecture. The discussion which will follow will be important and it's essential that I have an accurate short-hand report of it. Unfortunately, I can't entirely rely on Angela's accuracy."

131

She knew it was a statement designed to get a response from her, to make her take pity on him and say, "Yes, I'll go with you." She continued to gaze silently into the artificial flames. He sighed, but even that did not move her to speak.

Marisa's expression was stony and hard, a mask to disguise her feelings, her anguish and her desires. If she had so much as moved at that moment, he would have found her beside him, on her knees, her head in his lap, her arms groping upwards seeking for his and drawing them down to wrap them around her pliant body.

He broke the silence. "Have you been to the site lately?"

By 'the site' she supposed he meant where their house had once stood. She shook her head.

"They're excavating the foundations, so they've boxed in the whole area with hoardings to keep the public out. You wouldn't recognise the place now."

She said, her voice low, "I suppose there's a great gaping hole where the houses used to be?"

"Yes, there is. They're putting down the foundations. Do you know how they do it? They pour concrete into a kind of mould, like making a jelly. The mould — it's called 'shuttering' — has to be put up very carefully and they can't take it down until the concrete is quite hard."

"Does it take long?"

"To harden, you mean? About a month. Then it's tested, and if they think it's strong enough, they start building. I suppose you know I designed the office block they're going to put up on the site? I won't rub salt into the wound by showing you the plans." He looked at her with something that could have been interpreted as hope. "Unless you'd like to see them?"

It was her chance to do something she told herself she should have done years ago — show an interest in his work. She said, "Yes, please."

He was up at once and raking through his briefcase. He spread the plans on the table. "Come over here." She went to stand beside him. "You'll have to come closer than that. Don't be afraid," he mocked, "I'm not contagious. You can't 'catch' me."

She caught the double meaning as he had plainly intended she should. She pulled up a chair and he explained the different aspects of the design, putting into layman's language the technicalities she would otherwise have failed to understand.

"You see," he said, "first an architect must not only design, he must think of the construction in such terms that it will stand up." She laughed.

"It's true," he went on, smiling, "I've heard architects dismissed as 'romantics', who build not just castles in the air, but office blocks, flats and hospitals up there, too! People think that all we do is sit at our desks and draw pretty pictures, sketching plans which bear little or no relation to real life. They forget we're also intensely practical people, because we have to be, otherwise everything we design would fall down as soon as the builders have built it. You know," he elaborated, lost to his theme, and she thought with pride what a wonderful teacher he would make, "a design is really a piece of research. It can happen that a theory developed on the drawing board drives a designer one way, whereas a discovery on the site by the builders could stop the designer in his tracks and make him alter the original plans to suit the new circumstances."

They were both leaning on their elbows, their faces so close they were almost touching. Dirk turned and looked at her. "If," he said, "I'd done this years ago, if I had taken the trouble to explain my work to you ..."

The phone rang. He frowned and said, "Whoever it is I'll put them off. Don't run away."

The phone was in the hall and she heard him say, "Luella? Yes? Well, that's nice of you, but – er – I'm a bit involved at the moment. Work, and so on. Otherwise I'd have liked to come over. Sorry, my dear."

Marisa found her coat and pulled it on. "No, I haven't forgotten the theatre tomorrow. Yes, the matinée performance. Is Patrick looking forward to it?"

Marisa wrapped her scarf round her neck and pulled on her gloves.

"We'll have a meal together after the show. I've got tomorrow evening free." He glanced round and saw Marisa standing at the front door. "Must go, Luella. I'll pick you both up tomorrow. Goodnight, now."

He put the phone down and said, "Where the blazes are you going?"

"Home. Where else? Then you can go to your lady-friend. Don't let me stop you. I didn't invite myself here. You brought me."

He shrugged. "If you must go, I'll get my coat."

"I can go home by bus. No need for you to trouble."

"Come off your high horse, Marisa." He got into his coat. "And stop behaving like a jealous wife."

"That," she said hoarsely, "is the last straw! Here I am, tactfully getting myself out of the way so that you can go running into your girl-friend's arms, and you've got the cheek to call me a jealous wife!"

She wrenched open the door and ran down the stairs, but he caught her up and forced her to walk beside him to the car. They did not speak again until he drew up outside the house.

"Thank you," Marisa said, "for all the work you've done on the scenery. And for showing it to me. And for – and for the coffee."

"Anything else?" He sounded as irritable as she did. "You haven't exhausted the list yet, have you? And for showing you the plans, and for explaining them, and for being nice to you. Why don't you finish off like a good little girl who's been to a party and say 'Thank you for having me'? And you can take that whichever way you like!"

He drove away, leaving her standing at the kerb.

Two days before Dirk left for the conference, Jan invited Marisa to spend the evening with her.

"Neville's working late and I don't fancy my own company for hours on end. Let's have a nice girlish chat!"

Jan opened the door to her, shivering as a draught of cold air swept past her into the hall.

"Give me your coat. I decided to light a coal fire. Central

heating's all very well, but there are times when I like to roast instead of being just gently warmed through like left-over food!"

Marisa looked in the hall mirror and patted her hair. "Do you know it's over two months since I was here last?"

"So it is! With Elwyn on New Year's Eve. It's about time some buds appeared on the trees!"

Marisa sat on the couch beside some white knitting. "Talking of buds, what's this? A present for a mum-to-be? One of your friends?"

"No, dear, one of *your* friends."

Marisa's head came up. "Jan, not you?"

Jan nodded and Marisa's eyes filled. "Oh, Jan, I'm so pleased." They hugged each other. "When is it to be?"

"Late summer. So I'll be shaking the dust of Garner and Sterling off my feet before long."

Marisa asked, her eyes shining, "What do you want, Jan? Boy or girl?"

"We'll take whatever comes, we're quite open-minded."

"You're so sensible about it all! How could you keep it a secret like this? I would have wanted to shout it from the rooftops!"

Jan looked at her oddly and frowned down at her knitting. "Nothing you can do about it, dear?"

Marisa stared at the fire and leaned forward to warm her hands. "Nothing, Jan. I'm reconciled. I think this Luella woman's hit the jackpot where Dirk's concerned. He's almost part of the family now. After all, look at what she could give him – financial stability, even backing to start his own business if he wanted."

"But, Marisa, there's nothing he can do about it until he releases you. Why doesn't he agree to a divorce? Have you asked him?"

"Yes. He's made a condition."

Jan looked puzzled. "What condition?"

"Can't you guess? One more time, he said."

"But, Marisa, that's outrageous of him! It would be sheer hell for you. I never dreamed Dirk could be so – so sadistic. You refused, of course?'"

135

Marisa nodded. "I'm not made of stone, Jan. You know he's off in a couple of days to a conference? And Angela's going with him?"

"Yes, but I did hear that Angela's mother isn't too well. She's a widow and since there's only Angela at home now, there might be some doubt as to whether she can go with him."

Marisa said at once, "Well, I'm not going, Jan. He's already asked me and I've refused. Said I was a better typist, more intelligent and so on. Jan," she was appealing now, "I couldn't go with him. You understand, don't you? It would be an impossible situation."

Jan said she couldn't agree more. "Someone else will have to go. Marcia, for instance. Not terribly reliable, but he would just have to put up with that. Let's forget work, and talk babies. It's what's most on my mind these days!"

They spent the next hour chatting about domestic matters, then Jan made some coffee while Marisa sat on the kitchen stool and talked. They were about to carry the tray into the lounge when the front door opened. Jan brightened. "Ah, here's Neville. Just in time for coffee, darling," she called out.

"Got enough for four, Jan?" Neville asked. "Dirk's with me."

Jan's eyes opened and stared at Marisa. "I didn't know, dear, honestly. I'm sorry. Neville must have suggested it. I told him you were coming to keep me company. So blame him!" She answered her husband, "Of course, darling. Take Dirk into the lounge."

When Jan had added the extra cups to the tray, she led the way along the hall to join the others. Marisa followed her in. The two men rose, and Dirk stared.

"What are you doing here?" he said to Marisa. To Neville, accusingly, "You didn't warn me you'd have company."

Marisa pressed her lips together. 'Company', he called her!

"To be honest, Dirk, I didn't think it necessary to 'warn' you. Good heavens, man, she's your wife. I thought you'd be pleased to see her."

The situation was getting embarrassing. Jan said brightly, putting the tray down, "Told Dirk our news, darling?"

"He has," Dirk answered. "Heartiest congratulations, Jan." With his eyes on Marisa he added, "Nothing like a family to bind a couple together."

Marisa flushed deeply and Jan said with a wicked glint in her eye, "Rumour has it, Dirk, that you're going to acquire a ready-made family yourself, soon."

With a bright smile she handed him a cup of coffee. Marisa, beside her, held out a plate of cakes.

Now it was Dirk's turn to change colour, to an intense, angry red. "Who's been talking?" He looked at Marisa. "You?"

Neville, who was on the couch beside Dirk, rose and with irony motioned to Marisa to take his place. "If you're going to have a fight, do it within touching distance – unless you're going to use missiles!"

Dirk, realising that Neville was trying to save the situation, laughed. "Sorry, Neville. Come on, Marisa, sit down. We'll call a truce."

Marisa had to comply. They were guests and their hosts were their friends. Their own personal quarrel had to go underground for the moment.

"And what," asked Jan, drawing the conversation back to neutral ground, "have you two been doing this evening?"

"Working on Dirk's designs for the new office building," her husband replied. "They're good. I don't know if anyone's told you, Marisa, what a fine architect your husband is?"

Dirk cautioned, resting his hand on her arm, "Don't answer that question, Marisa. It's loaded. If you say 'yes', it will mean you're displaying a wifely pride you haven't got any more. If you say 'no', he'll immediately start to tell you, which in the circumstances would embarrass you horribly."

"I mean it," Neville persisted. "He manages to incorporate so many new ideas into the conventional framework that they're accepted by even out-and-out traditionalists without their even noticing."

"Thanks for the compliment, Neville," Dirk said. "If it's true, then it's only because I go around with my eyes open, noticing how others have coped with similar problems and using my own

137

imagination to improve wherever possible on their solutions."

"Is it possible," Jan asked, "to recognize the work of a certain architect in his designs?"

"Of course," her husband answered, "and his qualities and character, just as an artist can be recognised through the style of his paintings, and a musician through his music."

"So," said Dirk, with a provocative smile, "if you come across a building with a fierce, inhuman look about it, which ups and deserts its mate, you'll know it's mine. Isn't that true, Marisa?"

She laughed with the others and he shifted along the couch towards her. "I'm glad you know your faults," she said.

"One day," he muttered in a mock menacing tone, "I'll tell you yours, but be prepared to put a whole evening aside, because it will take all that time to list them."

The others laughed again, but Marisa, irritated now, moved away from him. Dirk, seeing the deliberate action, merely moved sideways towards her again.

"Watch out, Marisa," Neville said, "I think your husband has designs on you."

"You could be right, Neville," Dirk took him up. "One of these days . . . "

"Then," said Marisa, cutting in, knowing how closely Jan was watching them, "he must be looking at me through rosecoloured spectacles. My name's Marisa, not Luella, Dirk."

The shot went home and the smile was wiped from his face like a teacher cleaning the blackboard.

Sensing the tension, Jan held up her knitting. "Think it will fit Junior when he – or she – arrives?"

"If it does," Neville answered, helping her out in restoring the good-humour of the company, "he – she'll be a baby elephant!"

There was general laughter and drinks were poured out and handed round. It was getting late when Marisa rose to go.

"I'll run you home," Neville offered.

"Why," asked Dirk, "haven't you got your car here, Marisa?"

"No, I came by bus."

Dirk stood. "Don't bother, Neville, I'll give her a lift."

Neville shrugged. "As long as you can stop yourselves from

quarrelling while you're driving from this house to her flat!"

They did not speak on the way. Dirk seemed to have something on his mind. He drew up at the kerb and Marisa was about to leave him when he asked, "May I come in?"

His uncharacteristic humility, the fact that he, her husband, had had to ask to be invited into his wife's home, touched her so deeply she replied warmly, "But of course, Dirk."

There was an eagerness in her voice which, if he had been seeking encouragement, must have seemed as welcoming to him as arms flung wide.

The downstairs tenant appeared as they entered. She came through the door in the partition. She was a plump blonde in her mid-thirties, friendly and helpful. Her husband was a traveller and as he spent days and sometimes weeks away from home, most of her evenings were occupied in visiting friends.

Marisa introduced them. "Mrs. Scoby, my husband, Dirk."

Mrs. Scoby's eyebrows rose a little as her eyes examined him, then she smiled and said how pleased she was to meet him at last.

"I didn't know you were living here now," she said. "I'm out such a lot . . ."

"Oh, he's not," Marisa said hurriedly. "He's just called in for a few minutes."

"I see, dear." She spoke reassuringly, as if she quite understood. "Well," she waved, going out, "enjoy your chat."

They went upstairs and as they stood in the living-room, Marisa wondered what to say.

"Mrs. Scoby's a nice woman," she said at last.

"Yes," disinterestedly, "she looks pleasant enough."

There seemed to be something troubling him. He wandered round, staring at the Victorian paintings on the walls

"Good news about Jan and Neville's baby," Marisa offered tentatively. When would he tell her why he had come? She grew uneasy.

"Yes, very good." He turned and there was no friendliness in his eyes. "I suppose it's you who's been feeding Jan with those

139

tasty pieces of information about what is totally and exclusively my private business?"

Now she knew why he was there – to start another quarrel. He had not been able to pursue the subject during the evening, so he had stored up his resentment until he was alone with her.

"If you mean Jan's reference to your forthcoming alliance – I can't call it marriage, can I? – to Luella Ackland, the answer is yes, I did. But your 'business' as you call it is hardly private, is it, since you've made your liaison with her so public?"

"And you, of course," he sneered, "keep your liaison with Elwyn a secret."

"I have no 'liaison' with Elwyn. We're friends, nothing more."

"Don't be so damned hypocritical. I know otherwise."

She flared, "But you *don't* know otherwise! And what was that remark supposed to mean this evening about children binding a couple together?"

He smiled tauntingly. "I'm glad that shot hit the target. What I meant was that perhaps if you'd had a baby, we might still have been together. Who knows?

It was a question to which there was no possible answer.

He went on, "At least Luella bore her husband a child before he died. She has something to remember him by."

Now she was goaded beyond endurance. "How can you be so callous? You know we discussed it in the early days and decided to wait because we hadn't the money to give a child all we would want to give our own. You know we did. I wanted children. I still want a baby." Her voice grew strained. "Every time I see one I want to pick it up, nurse it, pretend it's mine . . ." Her voice tailed off, on the edge of tears.

Why was she telling him her most secret thoughts, this man of all people who, with such knowledge, could hurt her, taunt her even more than he did already?

"And I," he took her up, "the devil incarnate, am keeping you tied to me, preventing you from marrying Elwyn Worrell and thus fulfilling that dream. How you must hate me! Perhaps I should have given you a child before I left you. That at least would have assuaged your maternal longings."

She faced him, her lips trembling. "I didn't realise just how brutal you could be! And I thought I knew you. I once respected you as a man with the highest possible ideals, who was incorruptible, whose morals were beyond reproach."

"And now you don't." He thrust his hands into his pockets. "Well, all I can say is that you've grown up. You're seeing me at last as I really am, as unprincipled, as corruptible as the next man, who can abandon my moral values with the ease of everyone else these days."

"I never thought," she whispered, "that anyone could change so much in three years."

He did not answer her statement, but eyed her reflectively. He moved towards her, his head slightly down, and she backed away. "Don't worry, my *darling* wife," he sneered, "I have no intention of molesting you – yet." He stood still. "So you want a baby? The answer is simple – let Elwyn give you one. Why wait until you're free of me? Others don't bother about such niceties these days. After all, you'd get away with it, wouldn't you? You have a married name, my name, which the child could bear."

As he mouthed the unbelievable insult, her hand came up almost of its own volition and made stinging and vicious contact with his cheek. His eyes blazed, he raised his hand to strike her back and she cowered away. But even as his hand swung towards her, he checked it.

Her eyes, spilling over, told of the desolation within her. His arm went slack and fell to his side. He turned and walked out.

Dimly it registered on her consciousness that this had been yet another crisis, another deprivation. She wanted children, by her husband and no other, yet she knew it could never be. She had hit out, not just at him, but at life itself.

CHAPTER IX

NEXT morning Mr. Garner called Marisa into his office. He seemed uncomfortable and the reason became apparent at once.

He told her to sit down and eyed her over his half spectacles. "Mrs. Sterling, I shall come straight to the point. You know your husband is going to a three-day conference tomorrow? Unfortunately, Angela Smith, who was to accompany him, is unable to do so for domestic reasons. We asked Marcia Holland if she would be willing to go in her place. She agreed, phoned her parents for permission, but they refused. As she's under age – not yet eighteen – we have to accept the parents' decision. Since we cannot ask Mrs. Barclay, who is expecting a child, as you may know, you are the only typist left whom we can ask."

As Marisa drew a breath to protest, he held up his hand. "I'm aware, Mrs. Sterling, of what you're going to say, but I'm hoping you will put aside your personal objections on this occasion. Is there," he eyed her uncomfortably, as if the subject were distasteful, "is there no possibility at all of your coming together again with your husband?" He tutted as she shook her head. "Two intelligent, attractive young people, and yet you still can't patch up your quarrel?" He sighed. "But that apart, I'm asking you to go with your husband to the conference as an employee of the firm and as his secretary, nothing more."

"Mr. Garner," Marisa spoke at last, "does he – does my husband know you're asking me this?"

"We discussed it, naturally. He admitted that it was the only solution."

She wanted to ask, "What was his reaction? Did he get annoyed and make objections?" But Harris Garner, austere and unapproachable, was not the sort of man of whom one could ask such personal questions.

"Now, Mrs. Sterling, will you go?"

"Yes, Mr. Garner."

He sighed, this time with relief. The problem had been solved, neatly and tidily, and could be filed away. He got down to work at once. As she left him he said, "You leave tomorrow. It will mean packing a case tonight and making arrangements for all your domestic matters to be taken care of."

Marisa said she understood and returned to the typists' room. Jan, seeing her pale face, wanted to know what the trouble was now?

Marisa explained. "I couldn't refuse, Jan. He as good as said it was part of my duties to go."

"Which it is, of course," Jan agreed. "You'll just have to play it cool, dear, pretend Dirk means no more to you than any other man you might be going with to a conference."

Play it cool, after what had happened last night? Go with him all those miles, pretending there was nothing wrong, that they were friends instead of avowed enemies? The internal phone rang.

"For you," Jan said, handing her the receiver.

"Marisa?" It was Dirk. "Are you coming with me tomorrow?"

"Yes."

The conversation stopped abruptly with a clatter from the other end. No word of thanks, or relief, just silence.

She wondered if he would attend the rehearsal that evening. As usual, Elwyn took her to the hall and as they entered they saw Dirk standing beside Sally, his arm resting casually across her shoulders. He was laughing as though they had just exchanged a joke.

Sally waved and Marisa made herself smile. Dirk disengaged himself from Sally and stood, unsmiling, hands in pockets, watching the ritual of Elwyn taking Marisa's coat and putting it with his.

Sally called, "I've been trying to persuade Dirk to practise the kiss again, but he said it was too public!"

Dirk said, looking at Marisa, but talking to Sally, "I doubt if Elwyn requires another demonstration. He's no doubt getting plenty of practice himself with expert tuition from our producer."

Elwyn flushed and Sally's laugh rang out. "Now I know why he's getting so good at it!"

"Marisa," Dirk said, "I'd like a word with you." His voice was like lemon juice with just enough sweetening to take the edge off people's suspicions.

He motioned her to the door and she told the cast to assemble on the stage for a run through the second act. Then she followed Dirk outside. They stood in the entrance porch. Its light was dim, but not so bad that she could not see the hard lines on his face, the castigation in his eyes. So he had not forgiven her for what she had done to him.

His manner was brusque. "I'm not staying this evening. Everything backstage is under control and Norman can cope. I only came to see you about tomorrow. You know we're leaving straight after lunch in my car?"

"I didn't know, but I do now." She detected a sharp note in her own voice which she had not intended. He must have picked it up, because he became even more abrupt.

"You'll require sufficient clothing and so on to see you through three days. Two separate rooms have been booked at the hotel. One was intended for Angela and one for me." He paused and looked down at her in the weak light, his expression in shadow. "You realise you'll be accompanying me as my secretary and not as my wife?"

"Did you think," she asked quietly, "that I really needed that reminder? Or did you say it just to be unpleasant? Perhaps you would like me to revert to my maiden name while we're away so as to avoid any possibility of our relationship being misconstrued?"

He gave her a cutting look, opened the outer door, letting in the biting wind and went into the darkness.

Dirk did not have lunch with the others next day. When Marisa had finished her meal she asked Neville where Dirk was.

"Said he didn't feel like any food," Neville told her.

Marisa frowned and looked at her watch. "I'm supposed to be meeting him in the entrance hall at the office in half an hour."

On her way back she called at a dairy and bought milk and biscuits. If Dirk had not eaten he would be hungry long before their next meal, which she assumed would be dinner at the hotel.

She was waiting in the hall when he came down the stairs. His eyes were heavy, his face pale. He looked ill, but Marisa had to keep her anxiety to herself, not even daring to ask if anything was wrong. He took her case and the carrier bag she was holding and led the way outside.

They had been driving for some time, but he still had not spoken. Would he, she wondered unhappily, have treated Angela or Marcia with such contempt? Had he still not forgiven her for what she had done to him the other evening?

Unable to stand the silence, she asked, "When do you aim to arrive, Dirk?"

"Early evening. Dinner's at seven. From eight o'clock onwards there's a reception for the people attending the conference and their wives, if they've taken them, as some men do."

"But I, as your secretary, am not invited?"

For a moment she thought he was going to ignore her question. But at last he replied, "I doubt if I shall go."

Time passed and he still maintained his silence. They left one motorway and at a major junction joined another. She asked, "Aren't you hungry, Dirk? You missed your lunch."

"Is that a hint that you'd like to stop for a cup of tea?"

"No," she answered, bristling, "it was not a hint. It was a genuine question."

"Nevertheless, we'll stop at the next reasonable-looking café. And in answer to your 'genuine question,' no, I'm not hungry. I – haven't felt like food." It sounded as if he hated himself for making the confession. Her immediate concern communicated itself to him and, transferring his annoyance with himself to her, he snapped, "And don't go all wifely on me and get worried. It'll pass."

She took a few deep breaths to steady her voice and said, "Look, Dirk, let's have it out now. I didn't want to come. I wasn't even asked. It was implied by Mr. Garner that I was under an obligation to do so because I was an employee of the

145

firm. As I'm your wife – your *estranged* wife – you don't have to be considerate of my feelings. But I've come as your secretary, not your wife, so –" She looked at his hard, uncompromising profile and in spite of her efforts her voice wavered. "Don't you think you could at least be polite to me, if not pleasant? We're going to spend three days in each other's company. We can't go on like this." It sounded very much like pleading, and she supposed in a way it was.

He greeted her remarks with silence. So even his compassion had died with his love. It was getting dark when he drew into the forecourt of a café. "Come on, get out," he said, "you can have your cup of tea."

Marisa nearly whimpered, like a rebellious child, 'I don't want one,' but unfortunately she longed for one. Her throat was rough with dryness, her lips cracked from the pressure of her teeth.

In the café, Dirk sank on to a chair as though his legs would barely stand the weight of his body. Marisa was sure now there was something wrong with him. He drank the tea she poured out and, to her relief, took a biscuit, but even so he left half of it.

Back in the car he seemed to have to make an enormous effort to pull himself together. At the sight of his drooping body, she knew an aching fear.

"Dirk," she ventured, "let me drive."

He drew himself up. "It's nearly dark now. I'd better carry on." Then he glanced at her and she was glad the dusk prevented him from seeing her anxiety. "Would you drive? Would you mind?"

She was out of the car at once and standing at his door. He got his feet to the ground and she just restrained herself from putting out a hand to help him. He settled into the passenger seat and closed his eyes, his head resting back against the upholstery.

"Sorry about this. I feel terrible. I've been fighting it all day, but at the moment it's winning." She started the engine and he said, "You don't like night driving, do you?"

So he remembered! She tried to pass it off as a joke. "I always was a timid driver." She pulled out on to the main road and said, "The trouble is that my imagination goes out in front and sits on the bonnet tantalising me with all the terrible things that could happen if I made even the slightest error."

"You won't," he said, in the voice of a person on the edge of sleep. "If you're as much on your guard as that you should make a good driver, not a bad one. I remember when I started to teach you . . ." His voice faded away. He slept.

Now her fears came into their own, her hatred of driving in the dark, her concern for the man beside her, her apprehension about how they were going to pass the next three days together, in public keeping up the pretence of a friendly employer-employee relationship, in private reverting to their habitual animosity.

They were approaching the end of the motorway when it occured to her that she did not know where they were going. The petrol gauge showed that the tank needed filling so she pulled into the next service station and bought some petrol. Still Dirk did not wake. Marisa parked the car out of the way of others and found a map in the door pocket, opening it out wide and studying the area. But it was useless. She might as well use a pin, she thought, to decide where their destination might be.

As she folded the map her hand knocked against Dirk's arm and he stirred. His eyes came open and he blinked, finding the light which had been switched on in the car roof disturbing.

Marisa apologised for waking him and he stared at her as though she were a stranger. His eyes looked as though they could not focus properly and his cheeks were flushed. She put out a hand to feel his forehead, but he drew back irritably.

"I'm under the weather, that's all. Don't fuss." He looked round. "Why are we parked here?" She told him and he tutted. "I thought you knew where we were going. Why didn't you make it your business to know? You're supposed to be my secretary."

She suppressed her retort. "If you'll just tell me how to get there –"

"I'll take over. It's too complicated to explain."

"No, Dirk, you mustn't drive! You're not well enough.'

He opened the door and tried to stand, but sank back again on to the seat. "All right, but I'll have to stay awake to direct you. Prod me if I drop off again. And that's not a joke, it's an order."

She did not have time to resent his unpleasantness. It took all her concentration and driving skill to follow his directions and when they pulled up outside the hotel at which they were going to spend the next three days, she had to overcome her exhaustion and face the problem which was occupying her mind to the exclusion of everything else. And that was how to convince Dirk that he was too ill to be left alone. It was essential for her to be near him, at least within calling distance. He began to get out, but she said hurriedly, "Stay here, Dirk. I'll see about the bookings."

If she could persuade him to remain where he was perhaps she could ask the receptionist to change their rooms and bring them closer together. But Dirk would not be deterred, nor would he accept the support of the arm she offered. When they reached the brightly illuminated entrance foyer, she saw him clearly and was shocked by his appearance.

"You should see a doctor, Dirk," she murmured, but he brushed aside her suggestion. She said over her shoulder, "I'm going to try to get the rooms changed," and before he could remonstrate she was explaining the position to the receptionist.

"My husband is ill," she told the woman. "I've come to the conference in place of his secretary." Dirk reached the counter and sank on to the chair beside it, holding his head in his hands. The woman looked at him with sympathy. "Could you tell me," Marisa asked, "where the rooms already booked for him are situated?" She gave his name.

The woman studied the reservations book. "One on the first floor, and one on the second."

"Oh, dear. Would it —" She glanced at Dirk, who remained passive. "Would it be possible for you to change the booking and give us two rooms next to each other?"

The receptionist shook her head. "Not possible, madam, with

so many people staying here." She looked down a list. "There's been a cancellation of a double room. You could have that."

Uncertain now, Marisa asked, "Dirk? Would that be all right?"

He snapped, "Provided it has twin beds."

Marisa coloured slightly. The woman answered, yes, with twin beds, first floor. "Does that meet your requirements?"

"Yes, yes," said Dirk impatiently, "although I hardly see the need . . ."

The woman transferred her sympathy to Marisa, silently commiserating with her for having such a bad-tempered husband. "Number twenty." She handed Marisa the key. "I expect you'd like a hand with the cases?" She motioned to a porter who was standing near the door.

"Stay here, Dirk," Marisa said. "I've got the key to the boot."

He did not reply, but sat leaning forward, head down, hands clasped. She returned, holding the carrier bag while the porter followed with the cases.

In the bedroom, Dirk sank on to one of the beds. His body sagged under the weight of the illness, but his voice was vicious as he said, "Did you *have* to wish yourself on to me?"

"But, Dirk," there was surely some reasonableness left in him which had not been polluted by the illness, "I had to do it. You're ill, I'm still your wife, so it's my –"

"Yes, trot out that old one about your 'wifely duty'. I expected it." He held his head, then ran his hand through his thick hair. He looked up at her suddenly. "Had you forgotten that piece of paper we both signed legally separating us? It absolved you from all 'duties' towards me. You're under no obligation to care for me any more, either 'in sickness or in health'."

"But, Dirk, whatever I give you, whether it's my time, my attention or my compassion, I give of my own free will."

"Do you?" He raised his head and looked her over insultingly. "And what are you intending to 'give' me tonight?"

She had baited her own trap and fallen into it. She had asked for the insult and as usual, he had unhesitatingly given it to her.

He said, removing his coat and stretching full-length on the bed, "You'd better go down to dinner."

149

"Shall I ask them to send something up to you?"

He shook his head.

"I — I shall have to change, Dirk. Do you mind?" Marisa asked, hesitantly.

He forced out a laugh. "Do I *mind* if a woman undresses in front of me?"

She knew he was watching as she peeled off her dress but as she could not draw a curtain round herself, there was nothing she could do about it. She searched in her case and drew out a neat but attractive dark red dress and pulled it on. Then she ran a comb through her hair, catching it back with a slide. She applied a minimum of make-up.

Dirk was so quiet she wondered if he was asleep. His eyes were closed and she approached him quietly, hoping to remove his shoes without waking him. But he was not asleep. He allowed her to undo the laces and take off the shoes and she received a murmured "Thanks."

She moved towards his time, but his hand got there first. He smiled and this time there was no cynicism about it. He said softly, "You haven't really got designs on me, have you, while I'm in this feeble, defenceless state?"

She looked down at him, moved beyond words by the change in his manner. If he had shouted at her she could have withstood it, but his gentle mockery broke through her defences. He frowned at her tears.

"If you cry, I shall either think I'm about to die, or that you have some feelings left for me after all. Both of which would be wrong, of course." He closed his eyes again. "You'd better go down to dinner. While you're out I'll get into bed. And before you ask me, I don't want any food — none at all, so don't start arguing."

The large dining-room seemed to be full of men, although there were a few cultured-looking women among them. Most of them, Marisa assumed, had booked in for the duration of the conference. Near the curtained window a group of young women sat round a large table. They were secretaries, Marisa guessed. If she had not booked in as Dirk's wife, she would have been expected to join them.

She did not enjoy the meal, excellent though it was. Anxiety had robbed her of appetite. She wondered how to occupy herself for the rest of the evening. If Dirk wanted to sleep, which in his feverish state he should, she would have to leave him alone. The lounge was the only alternative, either reading or watching television. Neither appealed to her.

When she returned to the bedroom after dinner, Dirk was in bed and reclining against the pillows. His clothes were in a heap on the floor. Automatically Marisa picked them up, folded them and put them on a chair. He lowered the typewritten paper he was reading and watched her.

"What are you now – my wife, my maid, my nurse or my secretary?" His tone was impatient but a trace more amenable.

She smiled. "Well, since neither a maid, a nurse or a secretary would normally share a bedroom with you, I suppose I must be your wife." She looked at the papers strewn over the bed. "Should you be working? Shouldn't you be resting?"

"Yes," he nodded slowly, "definitely a wife, a nagging wife."

Her smile faded and she raked in the carrier bag. "I think you should at least have a drink of milk."

He shrugged. "If you insist. But no food, so you can put away those biscuits. Did you have a nice dinner?"

"Yes, thank you." She poured the milk into a glass and handed it to him. He drained the glass and returned it to her.

"Did you speak to anyone? There must be a number of people here I know."

"I think there were architects by the dozen, but I didn't feel sociable."

"So you didn't introduce yourself?"

"What as?" she asked sharply, washing the glass at the sink and leaving it to drain, "your secretary? It could hardly be as your wife, since you were so emphatic before we left that my real identity be kept secret."

"Well, it will have to be revealed now, won't it? I could hardly admit to sleeping with my secretary!"

She said stiffly, "I'm sorry for getting you involved with me like this."

151

"So am I," he replied, resting his head on the pillows.

She was about to retaliate when she saw the fatigue he was so valiantly fighting begin to have its way with him.

"Dirk," try as she might she could not keep the worry from her voice, "you must sleep. You're not well, however much you try to pretend you are."

"I've probably only got that accursed thing they call the twenty-four-hour 'flu," he said irritably, "so stop worrying and go downstairs. It's bad enough that I've got to have you in here all night without having to put up with you now, before it's really necessary. Behave like a perfect secretary and leave me to get on with my work."

She moved to the door, drooping and dejected.

"Marisa?" She turned a lifeless face towards him. "Where are you going?"

"You mean in case you should need me? The lounge, I suppose. Certainly not to the social gathering you said they've laid on. But don't worry, like a perfect secretary I'll come and listen outside now and then just in case you may be calling for me and wanting my services."

Before he could play with the final phrase like a dog having a game with a slipper, she left him.

The evening was lonely and long. She spoke to no one, despite the interested glances that came her way. She found a corner seat and stayed in it until she was almost dropping with fatigue – she did not want to be told again by Dirk that she was in the way – then she walked along the chill, dim corridor to the bedroom. The light was out and Dirk seemed to be asleep. She crept in, closing the door softly, and a voice said,

"I'm awake, so you can turn on the bedside lamp."

"Sorry if I disturbed you."

"You didn't."

The bedside lamp was well shaded, but in the darkness it shone like a beacon from a hilltop. She had been dreading the moment when she would have to prepare for bed.

As she slipped out of her dress she remembered with agonising

152

clarity the first night they had spent together, her shyness in front of him, his reserve which had touched her with ice, causing their first approaches to each other to be mechanical and self-conscious. But as the days had passed, so had their anxiety, and their feelings for each other had, with every expression of them, overcome their inherent reserve.

But the self-consciousness she had felt as a young bride was with her again. She was anxious and clumsy with her clothes and angry with herself for being so. She looked to see if he was still watching her. He had turned not just his head, but his whole body away from her. Part of her was relieved, but the other cried out in misery that she held no attraction for him any more. She supposed that after the heady wine of Luella, she, Marisa, was as uninteresting as a glass of water.

She got into bed, but it took her a long time to drift into sleep, and even then it was shallow and disturbed. It must have been in the early hours that he woke her, calling her name. She was out of bed at once and feeling her way, with the help of the moonlight whitening the walls of the room, across to his bed. Her hand reached out and made contact with his forehead. It was burning hot.

"What do you want, Dirk?"

"Nothing. Go away."

"But you called me. You're feverish. I'll have to give you something – a couple of tablets." She quietened his protests by saying, "If you don't take something to lower your temperature, you'll get worse and then we'll have to stay here together for a week, and we'd both hate that, wouldn't we?"

The last phrase sank in and had the desired effect. Dirk took the tablets and drank deeply from the glass she offered him. Then he turned away from her again. "Now go back to bed and leave me alone. For God's sake, get away from me."

Wearily she got back into bed, but sleep evaded her again. Was there no way of penetrating his barriers? Of course there was, but that road through to him was not open to her any more. Luella seemed to be the only one with a map, with a knowledge

153

of the terrain surrounding his tenderness and his love these days.

Dirk stirred and she was alert immediately. He moved again and it was an agitated sound.

"Marisa." The word came through the darkness as softly as a leaf caught up in a breeze. "I want you."

She half sat up, irresolute, shocked. "But, Dirk . . ."

"Oh," he was impatient, "not in that way. Good God, woman, I'm ill. I simply want comfort, nothing else." His voice was strained. "Let me hold you, Marisa. Are you quite heartless? You're a woman, you're still my wife . . ." He turned restlessly.

She went across to him, her heart pounding, her legs weak. She folded back the bedclothes and got in beside him. He moved slightly to make room for her in the narrow bed. His arms wrapped round her. She heard him sigh into her hair, heard the single word, "Thanks", felt him relax against her.

Surely, she thought, his fever would recede now. He was perspiring freely. It was the first sign, wasn't it, of the body's thermostat regulating the temperature?

At first she held herself rigid, but as his breathing deepened into a sleeping rhythm she relaxed, rejoicing in the feel of him, letting her love for him swamp her mind and body. It meant nothing to him, she knew, having her there. He was holding her as a tired child clutches a soft toy for comfort in the darkness.

At last she slept, too, and woke at first light, wondering where she was. With a shock she felt Dirk beside her. His hold had loosened, and as the daylight strengthened she looked at his face. It was tranquil. He was deeply asleep.

Holding her breath in case she wakened him, she eased herself out of his bed and replaced the bedclothes. He stirred and, still asleep, turned on to his other side.

She slid down into her own bedcovers, glad that she had not disturbed him. He probably would not even remember his request, and her compliance, in the early hours. He had been feverish, perhaps even dreaming. If he had found her there beside him, who knows what he would have thought of her, what construction he would have put on it?

She must have slept again, because when she awoke, he moved.

Marisa got out of bed and went across to him, her transparent flame-coloured nightdress revealing beneath it her shapeliness and the tinted whiteness of her skin.

He stared at her for a few moments, then closed his eyes as if he could not bear the sight of her. He was cool and pale. The fever must have left him overnight.

"You're looking better, Dirk. Do you feel it?"

"Yes, thank you." His voice was cool, too. "I'll get up for breakfast."

"But you can't, Dirk!" He opened his eyes and saw her concern, but it only seemed to make him more determined.

"Can't I? Try and stop me." He turned his back to her.

She put on the housecoat she had brought with her, took up a towel and sponge bag and went out to find a bathroom. The bath water was steaming hot and she returned to the bedroom flushed and revived.

Dirk was dressed and sitting in an armchair near the dressing-table. He did not look up as she entered, just went on reading the stack of papers on his knee.

Marisa dressed, hoping he was too absorbed in his work to notice. She sat on the upholstered stool in front of the dressing-table mirror and prepared her face for make-up.

He said, without raising his eyes, "Thanks for the touching act of self-sacrifice in the night. It was – appreciated." So he had not forgotten. He had been rational, his request had not been made in a spasm of fever. "I – er – noticed you escaped from me as soon as you decently could."

"It wasn't that, Dirk, it was –" How could she make him understand?

"All right," he cut in, "spare me the details. I appreciate how you felt. I'm no martyr, either." He paused, then went on, "And don't worry, it won't happen again. I wouldn't dream of taking advantage of your good nature a second time."

She applied her make-up automatically. He watched with a slightly cynical smile.

"Determined to put on a really good act, aren't you? The up-and-coming young executive's wife, faithful, loyal, devoted.

155

Dedicated to her husband's advancement by emphasising her own attractions, thus zealously enhancing his promotional prospects."

She parried his sarcasm and challenged him, "If you want to disown me, go ahead. As soon as we got down to breakfast – that is, if you're coming –?"

"I am."

"I'll leave you and go to the secretaries' table."

He looked down at his papers again. "You'll sit with me."

"I'm ready," she said tonelessly.

Dirk's footsteps were slow along the carpeted corridor. It was plain he had not made the miraculous recovery he thought he had.

He was recognised at once and surrounded by a circle of smiling people. Marisa was introduced to them all. She thought with cynicism, but with sadness, too, "They probably think we're the ideal couple, perfectly matched, deeply in love . . ."

A woman called Miss Platt introduced herself as "that rare breed, a female architect." She was middle-aged and perceptive and was the first to notice Dirk's indisposition.

"My dear Mrs. Sterling," she said, "should your husband be here? He looks so poorly."

"I agree with you, Miss Platt," Marisa said, "he's not well. I tried to persuade him to stay in bed, but –"

"I did feel ill yesterday," Dirk broke in, "but overnight I seem to have recovered somewhat, thanks probably," his eyes rested sardonically on Marisa, "to my wife's devoted attentions to my – er – needs."

Marisa met his gaze steadily until the mocking light in his forced her to look away.

"It's just as well," he went on, addressing Miss Platt, "because I'm reading a paper to the conference today."

"But, my dear man," Miss Platt protested, "I'm sure you're not fit enough to go up on the platform and deliver a lecture. Don't you agree, Mrs. Sterling?" She rested a hand on Marisa's arm. "Couldn't you turn on your wifely charm, my dear, and persuade this man of yours to stand down?"

Marisa coloured at her turn of phrase and was unable to meet Dirk's eyes.

Miss Platt drew in a breath as a thought struck her. "Mr. Sterling, why not get your dear wife to read the paper on your behalf? I'm convinced she has the necessary intelligence to interpret your words so as to gain the attention and sympathy of the audience."

Dirk frowned and Marisa protested, "But, Miss Platt, I'm not an architect. I'd make a terrible mess of it."

"No need for a knowledge of the subject, my dear. All you would have to do is to read the words in front of your eyes. With no disrespect to your husband," she smiled disarmingly at Dirk, "I would say that if you were to present the paper, even more attention would be paid to his ideas than if he were to present it himself. Certainly the gentlemen of the party would enjoy watching you!"

Dirk smiled because it seemed to be expected of him but said he would not hear of it. He had reckoned, however, without Miss Platt. She searched for allies, stretched out a hand and neatly captured a passing guest. He was young and long-haired and full of the all-knowing arrogance of the newly qualified.

"I'm sure you agree, Mr. Bryce," Miss Platt said, having explained the position to him, "that Mrs. Sterling would make an excellent substitute for her husband."

"Substitute," said Mr. Bryce, his eyes lingering appreciatively on Marisa's undeniable charms, "implies a certain inferiority, and I'm sure there's nothing inferior about Mrs. Sterling. You have only to look at her to realise that." And look at her he did, in detail.

"Now, now, young man," Miss Platt wagged a finger, "her husband is beside her. He can hear every word you say."

The young man turned to Dirk and smiled a superior smile. "Hasn't anyone told him that husbands are largely irrelevant these days? They're an expendable commodity." He returned pointedly to his contemplation of Marisa.

Dirk narrowed his eyes as if he were doing a rough estimate of the young man's weight and said, "Mr. Bryce, if you want to make love to my wife, go ahead." He paused. "But don't be surprised if I take you by the scruff of the neck and hurl you across the room."

The superior smile on the young man's face liquefied and ran away. Defeated, he turned and wandered off.

Momentarily thrown off course, Miss Platt frowned, but returned to her theme with greater vigour, adopting Dirk's moral victory as part of her campaign. "How I like to see," she said, "a husband using 'strong man' tactics to protect his wife. It appeals to the romanticist in me. Now, Mrs. Sterling, are you going to reciprocate by safeguarding your husband's health and deputise for him on the platform this morning?"

Marisa glanced uncertainly at Dirk.

"Come along, Mr. Sterling," Miss Platt rushed in, "it's all settled, surely? Confess that you really aren't fit to be up and about."

Dirk shrugged and appeared at last to be resigned to the situation. "You may be right, Miss Platt." He spoke on a sigh, either tired of the whole discussion, or perhaps secretly agreeing with the woman's summing up of his state of health.

Before leaving for the conference hall, Marisa and Dirk returned to their room. Dirk sank into a chair. The infection had receded, but it had not completely loosened its hold. Marisa sat on the bed, her legs a little shaky at the thought of the ordeal in front of her.

"If you'd rather forget the whole idea, Dirk, I don't mind. You could ask one of the other architects to read your paper. I'm not exactly looking forward to standing on the platform and delivering a learned thesis to all those people."

He replied wearily, "It's beside the point, isn't it, whether I object or not? It's clear I won't be fit enough to read the darned thing myself. You came as my secretary, so I suppose you're the obvious choice, but if you really haven't the necessary courage ..."

"Courage?" she cried. "Don't spare my feelings, will you?" She turned away. "Implying I'm a coward ... Must you be so unpleasant? Everyone else is being so kind."

158

He rose with an effort and rested his hand on her back. "Sorry. I'll try again. I'll put on the charm, shall I? Then you simply won't be able to refuse my request." His fingers tipped up her face and she saw a strangely touching smile playing round his lips. "Will you be the sweet, efficient secretary you usually are – we'll forget you're my wife for the moment – and read my paper to the conference? I know you can do it, I have every confidence in you."

She gave him a watery smile. "If you want me to, Dirk."

He sighed with exaggerated relief, squeezed her shoulder and moved away. "Thank goodness the 'charm' hasn't completely lost its magic."

At the conference hall next door to the hotel, they were shown to seats in the front row. Marisa allowed herself to glance over her shoulder and when she saw the great gathering of erudite-looking men and women, all of whom were experts in their own field, she thought with dismay of the ordeal she had to face.

Dirk must have sensed her fear. He bent his head and whispered, "What are you worried about? If the men get tired of listening to my ideas, they can keep themselves awake by contemplating the attractions of the woman who's addressing them!"

His praise, she knew, was calculated to inspire confidence, nothing else, but all the same she smiled at him with gratitude.

Until she was called to the platform, she worked without respite taking notes of the proceedings. Then there was a pause.

"Your turn next," Dirk murmured.

The chairman rose to make the dreaded anouncement. The next speaker, he informed the audience, should be Mr. Dirk Sterling, but he was unfortunately unfit and therefore unable to read his paper. However, his charming wife had kindly agreed to deputise for him and it was with pleasure – Dirk touched her hand and indicated the platform – that he now introduced Mrs. Dirk Sterling.

Marisa left the sanctuary of her chair and mounted the steps. The applause died down and when she dared to look up from the papers in her hand, the upturned faces below appeared expectant and interested. She sought desperately amongst the sea of people for her husband and his smile held encouragement and something else – it might, if she had not known better, have been mistaken for pride. She was immeasurably reassured by his silent support and made an immense effort to overcome her nervousness.

She spoke clearly and, as her confidence grew, her tongue dealt easily with the complicated technical terms the paper contained. At the end she was left in no doubt as to what the audience thought of her performance. She received the longest round of applause of the morning.

Limp with relief, her face flushed, she took her place beside Dirk again. He leaned across and whispered, "Well done!" and those two words held more reward for her than all the applause in the world.

For the rest of the day she worked steadily, taking notes of the discussions which alternated with the reading of papers. By the evening it was she who was battling with tiredness while Dirk, who seemed to have recovered some of his usual vigour, chatted animatedly with his colleagues. It grew so late she wondered if he was deliberately delaying the moment when they would be alone together.

At last, unable to maintain the show of sociability she had been putting on since dinner, she asked Dirk if he would object if she went to bed. He assumed an affectionate smile – for the benefit of his friends, she told herself bitterly – and said, "Of course not, darling," adding that he would soon follow.

She was almost asleep when he came in. He had disturbed her, but she tried not to let him know. It took him some time to wash and prepare for bed. She heard him turn back the covers and settle down with a sigh as if the day had been an effort to live through.

She murmured, "Goodnight, Dirk."

He answered tersely, "I thought you were asleep. Goodnight."

His tone of voice upset her and she found it impossible to sink back into the state of relaxation she had achieved before he came in. In the quietness her imagination turned the words into a rebuke and for a long time she fought with her tears and moved restlessly about the bed.

She heard a muffled question, "What's the matter with you? For heaven's sake, keep still!"

"Sorry," she answered, turning her face to the pillow to hide the waver in her voice, "I'm probably too tired to sleep."

She wanted to say, "Tonight it's I who need comfort. Why can't I ask you to come to me as I went to you last night?"

There was a short, brittle silence, then it was he who became restless. He switched on the bedside lamp, went across to the wash basin and drank some water. Her eyes were closed, but Marisa felt him pause beside her bed. Her heart hammered, her body tensed. Her eyelids lifted and their eyes locked.

"Dirk?" The word reached out to him as her arms longed to do. There was a question in her voice which he must have interpreted as fear, because even as she gazed at him his expression hardened. He swung away, turned out the light and appeared to settle down.

Distressed by his unforgiving attitude and spent with longing, she let the tears come silently, soothingly, until she sank at last into a deep, restoring sleep.

Next morning he was up before she stirred. In answer to her question he said abruptly, "Yes, thanks, I'm feeling better." She threw back the covers and swung her legs out of bed. He watched her for a moment, then went to the door. He was going out, he said. "For a breath of air."

"And to get away from you," he might have added, Marisa thought miserably.

At breakfast he told her, "We're leaving after lunch."

"But, Dirk," she protested, "the conference isn't over until tomorrow."

"By lunchtime today the most important part will be finished. I'm not spending another night here."

He did not add "with you", but the words were there, unspoken, implied. After lunch they left the conference hall, stopping in the town before heading north.

"I promised to buy something for Patrick," Dirk explained, parking the car near the shopping centre. "Coming?"

"No, thank you." Her tone was frigid.

"What about darling Elwyn? Doesn't he merit a present?"

His question was greeted with silence and he shrugged. When he returned he was holding two separate parcels. "One for Patrick," he said, putting it on her lap, "and one for his mother."

She picked them up, turned and placed them on the rear seat as quickly as if they had contained dynamite.

He smiled at her action. "What's the matter? Upset because I didn't buy you anything?" Marisa did not answer. "Remember you came in a secretarial capacity. You were paid by the firm for all the work you've done. After all," with a provocative smile, "a man doesn't give presents to his estranged wife, even if she has slept with him for the past two nights."

"You know that's only a half truth," she blurted out, "and anyway, the thought of a present from you never entered my head."

"And I know you're lying," he said softly.

When they drew up outside her home, it was dusk. He took her case from the boot and carried it to the front doorstep.

"I want those notes as soon as possible, Marisa," he said as he turned to go. "I shall have to study them carefully before making out the report."

She told him she would do her best. "Don't come to work tomorrow, Dirk," she urged. "You're still not properly fit, although you may think you are. And don't worry about the dress rehearsal tomorrow evening. Norman will be able to cope for one night."

Instead of thanking her for her thoughtfulness he remarked, "Thanks for your touching concern, but I shall go into work as usual tomorrow, even though it is against your advice. Don't worry yourself about my state of health, either. There's no need for you to go on acting the devoted wife. We're back to normal now." He added, his voice misleadingly soft, "And I can't tell you what a relief that is!"

CHAPTER X

The dress rehearsal had started when Dirk arrived. He stood beside Marisa for a few moments until there was a pause for the adjustment of someone's costume.

"Sorry I'm late," he said. She looked up at him and her half-smile turned into a frown of concern. However much he might deny it, he still looked tired. The lines under his eyes were dark enough to have been pencilled in by a make-up artist wanting to add years to his age.

"Go on, say it. I've already been told by a woman this evening that I look tired."

Her heart pitched forward like someone falling down a flight of steps. So he had called in to see his lady friend on the way to the rehearsal!

"Patrick was delighted with the present I bought him."

"And I suppose," she commented sourly, "his mother flung her arms round your neck in thanks for hers."

He straightened his tie with an elaborate movement. "Well," he smiled slowly, "I suppose you could say she did that. She wanted me to stay for a meal, but I said I'd already eaten and anyway you expected me here."

She said stiffly, "I'm sorry to hear your private life has been disrupted because of your obligations to me."

He looked at her with speculation. "Sarcasm? From you? What's biting you, Mrs. Sterling? It wouldn't be jealousy?"

She flushed. "Don't be stupid!" After a moment she smiled up at him. "I've finished typing those notes."

"What all of them?" She nodded. "My word, I always did say that for efficiency a certain secretary called Marisa Sterling was hard to beat."

She echoed his turn of phrase. "Praise? From you? What are you after, Mr. Sterling?"

"If I were you, Madam Producer," he drawled, his eyes narrow, "I shouldn't ask such a question." He left her and disappeared backstage through a side door.

The dress rehearsal proceeded with agonising slowness and indecision. So many things went wrong that even Sally seemed to be affected by last-minute nerves. As a consequence she did not give Elwyn the support he had come to rely on and his performance was slack and self-effacing at precisely the time when he should have been tense and self-assertive.

Philip, who was acting the part of an old man, forgot to slow down his actions, and instead of shuffling across the stage almost broke into a run. Judi was acting a plump, motherly housekeeper, but her padding in the vital places kept slipping out of position. Frances forgot her lines and Pete let his cigar burn too far and filled the hall with his shout as the heat touched his fingers.

Marisa mopped her brow. Dirk, who emerged from backstage rolling down his sleeves, saw the action and called, "Come on, everybody, cheer up the producer by giving her the 'all right on the night' routine."

"I think," said Patty, in charge of make-up, "it'll have to be stiff drinks all round before they go on stage tomorrow."

"Talking of alcohol," said Matt, "who's going to supply the necessary for the party after the final performance?"

"I'll bring a few bottles," Dirk offered.

"And me," said Norman. He looked round. "I take it between us we'll be able to provide sufficient food for the exhausted hordes to eat?"

Elwyn said his mother had promised to bake some cakes and Sally's mother had said she would make sandwiches and savouries.

"There you are, Matt," Dirk remarked. "No worries. That's the party taken care of."

Marisa turned to Elwyn. "Can you come back to my place and we'll run through your part again? You were a bit off-beat tonight. I must try to put you back on the track and there's only this evening left to work on it."

Dirk looked at her sardonically. As Elwyn went to get their

164

coats, Dirk whispered, "Inviting the leading man round to your flat? At this time of night? What else are you going to work on, besides the play?"

She turned on him. " 'Evil to him who thinks evil', as they say. Don't judge my private life by the way you conduct yours!"

She took her coat from Elwyn, put it on and swept to the door, out of range, as she thought, of her husband's retaliation. But she was wrong.

Dirk looked at his watch, saying loudly, "Still time to call on Luella. I doubt if she'll be in bed yet." He paused, then added, his tone calculatedly eager, "But it doesn't matter, it will be so much more – convenient if she is."

Marisa followed Elwyn out and left the door to slam itself shut. It had been a short, sharp exchange of fire and Dirk's had been the last – and most effective – shot. The skirmish had ended in a rout and she was the vanquished.

Marisa woke up next morning feeling apprehensive. She had to acknowledge she was suffering from a large dose of producer's first-night nerves. A few more hours and her weeks of effort would be put to the test. All the tickets for both performances had been sold. Elwyn's mother and aunt were going to be there and so, it seemed, was Luella.

Marisa travelled to work by bus, leaving her car in the garage. The passengers filed off in front of her and, still wrapped around in thoughts about the play, she did not see the car that was cruising along the road beside her. When she heard her name called, she looked up.

"Where were you?" Dirk asked, opening the door for her. "As if I didn't know. At tonight's performance, I suppose. Where's your car?"

"At home. It's taken to stalling at traffic lights and cross-roads, which is embarrassing."

"You should have it serviced."

"It's so old I'm wondering whether it's worth spending any more money on it. Things are going wrong with it one after the other and now the heater's packed up, which in this weather isn't very pleasant. I wish the spring would come. Thank goodness it's almost the end of March." She settled back in her seat. "In the bus just now I could see the hills in the distance. The sight of them was enticing, although some of them are still covered in snow." She closed her eyes, visualising them. "I must get away from the town soon and go up on the moors again. I'm not waiting much longer, snow or no snow."

"What's the attraction – the wide open spaces?"

"Perhaps. I'd like to try and find the inn where we spent our honeymoon." She regretted the words at once, knowing he would follow them up with a question she could not possibly answer.

But he didn't ask why. Instead he looked at her obliquely and said, "Tell me when you're going. I might come with you. Who knows," he turned cynical, "what magic it might work on us? But even if it did bring about a reconciliation, the magic wouldn't last, would it, any more than it did last time?"

"No," she answered dully, "not without the one vital ingredient."

"Which is?"

"Love."

Dirk turned into the car park and they walked in silence to the office, to part without another word at the foot of the stairs.

The hall was filling and the subdued, expectant chatter of the incoming audience was communicating itself to the actors behind the scenes. The tension was building up. They were all in various stages of nerves, dress and make-up.

Anna was running from one dressing-room to the other, fussing over costumes, squabbling with Patty who was trying to apply make-up or supervise the actors' own application of it, in between Marisa's last-minute advice and Matt the stage manager's instructions.

Dirk and Norman had already lifted the first scene set into position and were manoeuvring the next lot of scenery into a better place for a quick change. Sally was the most composed

166

of all. She hung around Dirk asking him to admire her and tell her how much older she looked in her stage make-up.

"Old enough to be your girl-friend," she said, her lips hovering near his.

Dirk repulsed her gently but decisively. "You're too late. I told you, I've already got one."

Sally turned to Marisa, appealing to her, "Has he really got a girl-friend?"

"Yes," was the flat, toneless answer. "She's here tonight. Her name's Luella."

"She's right," Dirk said, grinning at Marisa. "And, as I said before, she's rich. Not only that, she's beautiful. So you see, young Sally, you don't stand a chance."

Sally pouted. "If I really got going on you, you wouldn't stand a chance. You wouldn't be able to say 'no' to me."

Dirk laughed, enjoying the joke. "You're wrong, you know, quite wrong." He glanced at Marisa. "I'm the faithful type. I never let down the woman I love."

"I doubt," Marisa said icily, "whether you have the capacity to love any woman. Or to be faithful to her if you did."

Dirk's eyes slitted. He confronted Marisa, hands on hips. "You're not, by any chance, challenging my statement, are you, Madam Producer?"

"Lighting's fixed," said Norman, joining them, and to Marisa's relief making an answer to Dirk's question unnecessary. He looked at his watch. "Fifteen minutes to go. Right, Marisa? Coming, Dirk?"

The performance went without a hitch and was received by the audience with thunderous applause. There were half a dozen curtain calls, which delighted the cast, followed by shouts for the producer. Flushed with pleasure and relief, Marisa allowed herself to be persuaded by the others to go on to the stage for a few moments. She bowed deeply left and right and the applause rose to a crescendo. The curtain fell for the last time that evening.

Sally, unlike the others, came out of the ordeal as full of life as she had been at the start. Her joy of living was only temporarily tarnished by the appearance behind the scenes of Luella Ackland, who seemed to be waiting for Dirk to take her home.

Marisa felt that, as the producer, it was her duty to speak to Luella, but her friendly approaches to the woman with whom her husband appeared to have fallen so deeply in love were received with such studied frigidity that Marisa felt her own features, on which the cold eyes had momentarily rested, had begun to suffer from frostbite.

She turned away and saw with delight that Jan and Neville had come to seek her out. They congratulated her on the production and with a movement of the head, drew Marisa's attention to Dirk's "rich widow."

"I know," Marisa whispered, "I tried to make contact with her, but –" She finished her sentence with an expressive shiver.

"I tried talking to the woman in the interval," Jan commented under her breath, "and got the same reception."

"Dirk says she's beautiful," Marisa murmured despondently.

"Luella *beautiful*?" Neville asked hoarsely. "Where's the beauty in a woman chipped out of a block of ice? I should think her husband died as a result of prolonged exposure to her Arctic temperature! How Dirk can fancy her remoteness after the flesh and blood warmth of his wife –!"

Dirk appeared, pulling on his coat. He went at once to Luella. Then he spotted Jan and Neville and took Luella across to join them, but she stood apart while they all discussed the play. "Dirk's friends," her ice blue eyes seemed to say, "are not my friends."

Hester Worrell and her sister Florence came self-effacingly backstage and Marisa went to greet them.

"Hallo, dear," said Mrs. Worrell, moving her stick to her left hand and with her right pulling Marisa's face down to kiss it. "Lovely play, dear. You did well." She nudged her sister, pointing at Dirk and whispering, "That's him." Then she said, deliberately raising her voice, "No wonder Elwyn's so proud of you. He's so fond of her, isn't he, Florrie?"

"Very fond, dear," Florence agreed loudly, eyeing Dirk with distaste. "He's always talking about you."

They spoke so loudly Dirk could not have failed to hear. Marisa stole a look at him only to meet his derisive smile.

Mrs. Worrell caught sight of Elwyn, attracting his attention by waving her stick. "You were grand, son," Hester said to him. "And I liked that little girl you played opposite. Lovely, she was. And I do think Marisa's so clever to be a producer." To Marisa, "Coming home with us, dear?"

Marisa hesitated, her glance going instinctively to Dirk. But he had not been listening. He was talking to Luella and bending his head to catch her reply.

Marisa said with decision, "Thank you, Mrs. Worrell, it's very kind of you. I'd only be alone, otherwise."

"It's not kindness," Hester Worrell answered, moving slowly towards the door. "It's only what you deserve after all that work. I'll make you a nice cup of tea. I expect you'd like that, wouldn't you?"

Marisa nodded, grateful for the woman's kindliness and comforted by her consideration. For once she did not resent Elwyn's possesive attitude. After watching Dirk's studied attentions to his rich client, it was like a balm to her injured pride to have Elwyn fussing over her and to listen to his extravagant praise of her skill as a theatrical producer.

The second performance of the play was even better than the first, and the audience was, if anything, more appreciative. When the curtain came down for the last time, Sally ran round hugging everyone, and even Elwyn relaxed sufficiently to hug her back. Then the men dispersed to their dressing-rooms to remove their make-up and change for the party, while the women did likewise in theirs.

Marisa slipped off her trousers and sweater, packing them away in her suitcase and took down from a hanger the dress she had brought with her. It was the dress she had worn for the firm's annual dinner. She knew it would provoke sarcastic comments from Dirk, but tonight she just didn't care. There was an odd sense of excitement inside her which, however hard she tried, she could not rationalise away. In the end she accepted it as part of the elation she was feeling at the success of the play and the culmination of weeks of hard work.

The party took place on the stage with the curtains closed. The hollow sound of the boards beneath the feet, the flies overhead into which the scenery was hoisted and stored, the wings leading offstage and the heavy drape of the curtains, gave an artificiality to the atmosphere which the others seemed to revel in, but which Marisa felt with apprehension.

The movements, speech and laughter of the people around her were infused with a dreamlike quality, as though the play was continuing without an audience, without a story even, as if they were all characters who existed in a playwright's mind and were not real people any more.

Sally had attached herself to Dirk and he was looking down at her, glass in hand, half amused, half detached, listening to her chatter.

Elwyn gave Marisa another drink and offered her a sandwich. "I missed my tea," she said.

Dirk heard her and strolled across to join them. "Me, too," he commented, "so that makes two hungry people on this stage." His eyes tried to net hers, but like a wily fish she slipped through the mesh.

But he pursued her. "You're wearing that dress again."

She looked at him this time. "What of it?"

He raised an eyebrow. "Asking for trouble?"

"I don't know what you mean."

"You know perfectly well what I mean."

Elwyn might not have been there. To this man and woman who were husband and wife he had, for a few seconds, ceased to exist. He had been momentarily written out of the script by the playwright. He did not like being treated as though he had no substance, so he said,

"I think she looks great in it."

Dirk unravelled his eyes from Marisa's and turned his attention to her companion. "You know, Elwyn, you're right. She looks superb in that dress. It whets my – er – appetite." He looked Elwyn over, noting with apparent satisfaction his reaction and the jealousy it contained. "You look very formal, Elwyn." His tone was baiting. He glanced down at his own clothes, patterned shirt, floral tie, fitted cord jacket, casual close-fitting trousers. "Unlike me, you still stick to conventional styles as though the new fashions didn't exist."

Elwyn answered sulkily, "My work demands it."

"But you're not at work now, which can only mean that you accept the formality imposed on you. Otherwise you wouldn't have dressed in such a sober suit and tie for a party like this. You would have broken away, as I have."

He took two drinks from the tray Anna offered him and gave one to Marisa. The other he kept for himself, omitting Elwyn, thus putting him in his place as an onlooker and an interloper.

"This," said Marisa, holding up her glass, "is my fourth."

"If I'd known that," Dirk said, "I wouldn't have given it to you. You'd better not have any more. You're not used to it."

She resented his dictatorial attitude and rebelled. "I can drink as much as I like."

Dirk's eyes narrowed. "Just remember that this is not stage wine. It's the real thing. And it's potent." She gazed back at him boldly and tipped the contents down her throat.

He smiled at her blatant challenge, and regarded her estimatingly, half-closing his eyes. "If you finish up under the table, Madam Producer," he drawled, "don't expect me to come and pull you out." He lowered his voice still further. "If you provoke me much more, sweetie, I'll even come and join you there."

The wine was affecting her strongly now, and she gazed back at him, her eyes wide, her lips parted, only half aware of how she might be encouraging him.

He detached his eyes from hers and returned, like a champion boxer playing contemptuously with an inexperienced opponent, to his harassment of Elwyn. "If I, as an architect, were to cling to the old ways as you cling to old fashions, I'd still be designing Victorian houses with turrets and pointed gables and no bathrooms. Enormous living-rooms, too, which once had a function – to accommodate the large families of that period. I'd be plan-

171

ning servants' quarters, regardless of the fact that there are no servants to live in them any more."

Elwyn shrugged. "All right, so I'm a bit old-fashioned. I like the old ways. Each to his own." He moved closer to Marisa and put his arm round her.

Dirk saw the action which this time cleverly excluded him. He said, his eyes cold, his tone barbed, "One man's meat..." His glance ran insultingly over Marisa. "You can finish the rest of the proverb yourself, Elwyn." He turned away and joined Norman and his fiancée.

The record player was beating out music, the conversation rose to drown its noise. The cigarette smoke fanned out across the stage, drifting away into the wings. Plates became empty, bottles ran dry.

Elwyn was deep in a discussion about the play with one of the other actors. Marisa was alone. Her eyes sought out Dirk, who was standing diagonally opposite her across the stage, near the footlights. He must have felt her looking at him because his eyes lifted to meet hers.

The impact was physical, as if he had touched her. They gazed at each other. The noise waned, the others faded, blotted out for a handful of seconds by the playwright's mind. It was as if there were only two characters left to act out the drama — herself and Dirk. She let out her breath, but caught it again as he began to move, weaving a tortuous route between the others, towards her.

He stood in front of her. He said softly, "Hallo, Marisa," as if they were meeting for the first time that evening. She swayed back against the curtains seeking support, but in their yielding limpness finding none.

He raised his glass and over the rim of it his eyes, in shadow by a trick of the lights, held a question. He whispered, " '*Drink to me only with thine eyes, and I will pledge with mine.*' Tell me what comes next, Marisa."

She quoted softly, obediently, " '*Or leave a kiss within the cup and I'll not ask for wine.*' "

He took up the poem, " '*The thirst that from the soul doth*

ise doth ask a drink divine...' " His fingers reached out and
ipped up her face. "Marisa?" The word was questioning,
urgent.

The music had changed to *Greensleeves;* the melody was
evocative, the past stirred to life within her like the return of
spring after a long and endless winter. She was barely conscious
of the 'yes' she gave in answer to his question. She did not speak
the word, there was no need. It was there, in her eyes.

"Dirk, *Dirk!*" Sally was pulling at his arm and, like someone
whose sleep had been disturbed, he roused himself and turned.

"They keep telling me," Sally said, "my lipstick came off
on Elwyn." She had only lightly removed her stage make-up.
Most of it was still on her face. "I don't believe them. You kiss
me, Dirk, and see if it does come off." She held out her lips.

He put down his glass and kissed her experimentally, his
hands resting on her shoulders. Then he got out his handker-
chief and wiped his lips. The white material was stained with
red.

"They're right," cried Sally, "it does come off!"

He stuffed his handkerchief into his pocket and turned. There
was a light in his eyes which made Marisa back away, but there
was no escape through the dark folds of the curtains.

"I wonder," Dirk murmured, moving purposefully towards
her, "if our producer's lipstick comes off. Does it, Marisa?"

He gave her no chance to answer. She was caught by his
arms, and his lips, so familiar yet so alien, came down and ex-
pelled the breath from her body.

From a distance, like someone shouting across a desert, Mar-
isa heard Sally squeal, "Dirk, *stop it, Dirk!*" But Dirk did not
stop. "Look what he's doing, Elwyn!" There was anguish in
Sally's voice because she saw that what she wanted for herself
was slipping away out of reach like a boat broken loose from its
moorings. "*Do* something, Elwyn. She's your girl, don't let him
steal her!"

But only Elwyn knew what was really happening and only
Elwyn knew how powerless he was to bring that kiss to an end.
But end it did, at last, and as they drew apart Norman said, his

173

arm round his fiancée, "I knew she'd catch you, Dirk. I did warn you, didn't I? But you didn't run fast enough!"

The others laughed, as if glad of a joke to relax the oddly tense atmosphere.

Dirk said quietly, abruptly, "Get your coat, Marisa, I'm taking you home."

In the dressing-room she put on her coat and picked up her case. Her legs were unsteady, her thoughts confused. Whether it was the wine that had intoxicated her or the kiss which still lingered on her lips, she did not know, but she was not completely in command of her own actions.

When she joined Dirk on the stage, he too was dressed to leave. The others waved and wished them luck. Dirk took Marisa's case and they could have been a couple going away on their honeymoon.

Only Elwyn stood motionless, his envious eyes watching his rival take the prize, as a poor man watches a rich man drive away with a car he had coveted but did not possess the money to buy.

The journey to Marisa's flat was silent. The tension between them stretched and pulled, binding them together like a rope between climbers. She led the way upstairs. In the bedroom she took off her coat and turned to face Dirk, trying to read his thoughts from the expression in his eyes, but they were unfathomable.

She waited, tolerating his gaze which ranged over her like a mountaineer assessing in the closest detail the pinnacle he was soon to scale. His arms reached out and she fell into them, pliant, willing, powerless to oppose. He contemplated her radiant face as a deep sea diver looks momentarily at the water before plunging in.

"You, my sweet," he whispered, "are not entirely sober." With a jerk she was against him and cradled in his arms. "I'm staying," he said, and his mouth came down.

Slowly, slowly, under his caresses she yielded until her body was totally compliant and not a trace of resistance was left to hinder his advances. His lips trailed her neck, her face, her mouth,

174

and she became caught up in his desire and was folded into him. Long-forgotten sensations were recalled, shared delights remembered, and as the time passed and their knowledge of each other's needs returned, so the intensity of their pleasure grew. His joy was hers, his ardour received and reciprocated.

He took her gently, with tenderness, then with mounting passion, and her last rational thought before she succumbed entirely was, "He still loves me."

Once in the night she stirred and found his arms were round her and she was filled with the deepest contentment she had ever known.

When she woke in the morning she was alone. He had gone, but it did not worry her. It was Saturday and he would come back. She washed, dressed and made the bed. She had some breakfast and washed up.

Every time she looked in the mirror it showed her a woman with brilliant eyes, ecstatic, elated. Dirk had come back, and now she possessed his love as never before, not even in the early days of their marriage. The legal document they had signed would be torn up. Nothing would come between them ever again.

She went into the living-room to tidy it, and it was then that she saw the note. It was propped up in front of the clock. It said simply, "Marisa". Her heart already beating fast, began to hammer and the hand reaching out was shaking, as if suddenly possessed of the power of foretelling the future.

"Thanks", the note said, "for the night's entertainment. You certainly earned your reward. Now you've complied with my condition you can have the divorce you keep pestering me for. That's why you did it, isn't it? – Dirk."

The note became a crumpled unreadable ball in her hand and it hit the empty grate, rolling a little drunkenly before it finally came to rest.

Marisa closed her eyes and swayed. Using her hands to guide her, she moved round the furniture and found the way to a chair. She felt sick, humiliated, and wanted to die. It was like an illness, this feeling in her limbs, as though she had been struck down with a terrible disease, one from which she would never recover.

She held her head and tried to cry, but her eyes were burning and nothing would come. Her lips were cracked and stiff. They moved as if speaking, but no words came out. Her breath was short as though she had been racing up an endless flight of stairs, her eyes could see but were not seeing. Her brain could function, but its powers of reasoning were dimmed.

She was suffering severely from shock, and it was taking command of her body, seeping through her insidiously, debilitating her limbs, contaminating her mind and lighting a furnace behind her eyes.

She told herself she had to get away. She would go up on the moors and over the hills to find the inn where they had spent their honeymoon. If she could get there she would be back in the past, she would discover that the last three years were nothing but a nightmare which had never really happened.

She dressed in sweater, trousers and boots. She pulled on her anorak, fastening it and tying the hood under her chin. Food? she wondered. No, a bottle of milk would be sufficient. Her actions became feverish and she began to hurry as though there was no time to waste. The past was calling her and she must not keep it waiting.

In the hall she met Mrs. Scoby. "Off out already, dear?" asked Mrs. Scoby.

"Yes," Marisa answered, her voice high and toneless like that of a sleepwalker, "yes, I'm going out. To the moors. To find . . ." To find what? The past. But Mrs. Scoby wouldn't understand. An inn. That's it! "To find – an inn." Seeing the other woman's keen, probing glance, she sought for a moment's rationality and steeled herself to smile. "Must get some air, must get away from the house for a bit."

"But, dear," Mrs. Scoby urged, "it's cold, the weather's nasty. I should wait, love. Till the spring. It won't be long now, will it?" Her voice, humouring, soothing, as though she were talking to a whimsical, slightly off-balance child, frightened Marisa, who shook her head violently and then ran back out to the car.

It fired at the third attempt and she was away down the road and through the town, making for the open moorland as though the car was running on rails, on a predetermined course, as though it knew the way by instinct and was taking her there of its own accord.

She noticed the clouds gathering like soiled cotton wool overhead, but the sight aroused no apprehension as it would have done had she been in a normal state of mind.

Somewhere in the centre of her brain red lights flashed, red for danger, but she understood their meaning no more than man understands what is in the centre of the earth. The roads were icy and, had she been rational, this would have terrified her, but the everyday fears which usually haunted her had no power to touch her now.

She was as distraught and unbelieving as if the man she loved had died. But it was true, wasn't it? The man she loved did not exist any more. The man who had written that note was a stranger, an insulting, sadistic stranger. And that was why she was running away, to find the man she had married. He was up there, she was sure, waiting for her to come to him.

She drove mechanically and as the miles passed and the moors opened out, the traffic lessened until there was no other vehicle in sight. She had reached the snow line and the touches of white on the distant hills – those hills which had looked so attractive from the windows of a bus – were now a daunting, icy, white sheet laid across the barren land around her.

The road flung into the far distance like buckled brown tape. It drew her on, beckoning, enticing her towards her goal. The snow began, gently at first, no even needing the windscreen wipers to sweep it away. But even when the fall increased it did not deter Marisa. She simply did not notice. Her eyes were fixed on the road ahead, disregarding the sheep which browsed and plodded and bleated, comforting the young lambs, sheltering them with their bodies from the biting wind which drove the snow in horizontal lines over the moorland and across the path of the small red car.

It did not occur to her that in such conditions it was madness to carry on. She left the main road and the gradient became sharper, the hills on each side assuming a menace of their own. But there was no room in her mind for fear. Her objective, her absolute conviction that she would find the man she had married at her journey's end drove out all other feeling.

She still had miles to go. The road fell away, only to climb again, until she was driving almost parallel with the summits of the hills which, lower down, had seemed so remote.

She came upon the inn suddenly as she topped an incline. It stood in isolation, its outer walls made of the grey stone which abounded in the land around it. She drew up outside and there seemed at first to be no sign of life. Then a child put his head round a half-open wooden door, stared, and disappeared, probably to announce the arrival of a stranger.

Marisa stayed in the car for a few moments, watching the snow coming to rest on the bonnet, only to melt at once from the heat of the engine. The enormous silence of the hills began to penetrate her consciousness where no sound could make any impression.

She opened the car door and, still like a sleepwalker, trod a path in the snow to the front door. It was opened before her knuckles could make contact. The kindly face of a woman smiled at her. Surprised, the smiling face said, to see someone up there in this terrible weather. Something wrong? Trouble with the car? A meal?

"A man," Marisa said, and even to herself her voice seemed weak, "a man, her husband, was he here?" She described him as he had been five years before.

The smiling face grew serious and frowned. No, it said, no man had been up there, no one for days. "In this weather we don't expect anyone, except perhaps an occasional tradesman delivering supplies."

Marisa's face crumpled like a disappointed child. The woman grew anxious. Must have been some mistake, she said. "Come in, love. I'll make you some lunch. Have you come far?"

"Yes," Marisa told her, "miles and miles."

"You shouldn't go back all that way in this. It'll get worse, miss, before it gets better. Sometimes we're cut off for weeks. Come in and stay a while."

"No, no," Marisa said, her voice as thick as the blanket of snow being laid so gently and so lightly over the hills, as if across an invalid. "No food, thanks, no meal. Must be on my way." She thanked the woman again and returned to the car to begin her journey back.

Drifts were piling up against the drystone walls, driven there by the wind. A snow mist was descending and the sheep, wandering restlessly, became part of the whiteness of the landscape. The sky was leaden, threatening even heavier falls.

In her dull, unresponsive state her reactions were slow and she did not see the lamb which was standing in her path until she was almost on top of it. She swerved violently and the car went into an uncontrollable skid. It came to a stop, unbelievably the right way up, but broadside across the road. The lamb ran away to find its mother.

Marisa slumped over the steering wheel, her cold-stiffened fingers gripping the top of it, her head resting on her arms. There was everywhere the profound moorland silence and an infinite, limitless white loneliness. A sheep bleated, then another, and then nothing.

She roused herself, switched on the ignition, but the engine stalled. She tried again and it went on stalling until there was no response at all. The battery, in need of replacement like most of the car's components, had petered out.

A remnant of common sense asserted itself and she realised how dangerous it would be to leave the car straddling the road, even though it was unlikely that any vehicle would come that way for hours, if not days. She got out and with one hand on the steering wheel tried to guide and push the car at the same time. But the snow was too deep and her strength was not equal to it. She walked around, hands in pockets, too cold even to shiver. Her mind was growing snowbound, too, cut off from reasoned thinking. She got back into the car. She had no blanket, no gloves, no covering except her clothes which, in the freezing temperature high up in those snowey hills, were barely adequate.

Dimly she remembered the milk she had brought with her. She got in the back of the car, found the milk and drank it. The liquid was icy cold and her teeth and throat throbbed with the pain of it. The bottle dropped to the floor and she slumped face down across the back seat, her head resting on her arms.

The snow fell thicker and faster, piling up against the car until in time it almost covered the windows. As consciousness slipped away, it was a little like dying. It would be so easy to die, so simple to leave all her misery behind. Something tried to tell her that the last thing she should do was to succumb to the desire to sleep, that she should keep moving and exercising, forcing the blood to remain active and flowing in her veins, and that to stay still and sleep was courting death. But she ignored all the warnings and welcomed sleep – and its consequences – with open arms.

CHAPTER XI

A bottle was being pressed against her clenched teeth, a hand was under her head, raising it a little. A voice said, "Drink, for God's sake, drink!" Some of the liquid penetrated the barrier of her teeth and ran over her tongue and down her throat. It burned and she gasped and coughed and choked, struggling to get away from the person who was forcing her to drink against her will.

She had nearly died, she had so nearly achieved her objective. Now there was someone reviving her, bringing her back to the life she had wanted to throw away. Whoever it was seemed satisfied with her response and removed the bottle. Then her hands were being rubbed, her boots taken off and her feet and ankles chafed. Still she did not open her eyes. Someone was lifting her out of the car and carrying her over the snow, putting her down on a hard floor and wrapping a blanket round her. A pillow was placed under her head. She tried opening her eyes, but it seemed to be dark everywhere, although through the opening of a door – she seemed to be in some sort of vehicle – there were the remnants of daylight. She sank back and lay motionless.

"Drink this, Marisa." At the sound of her name, at the abruptness of the voice, she lifted her head and in the light of a torch she saw a man. As his face, lined and worn, came close, she shrank away. It was the stranger who had written that note, destroying her happiness and making her want to die.

He put his hand under her head, but life was returning now and she twisted away. "This is hot, Marisa. It's tea from a flask." The voice sounded fatigued, resigned. "You *must* drink it, otherwise you won't survive."

"I don't want it," she whispered.

"My dear Marisa," he sounded tired beyond words, "however

181

much you may hate me, I'm not going to let you die on me, so drink!"

She drank, her need for sustenance getting the better of her, then she sank back with relief on to the pillow. "Where am I?" Her voice was high-pitched and colourless.

"In a Land-Rover."

"Why did you come?" There was no answer, no sound but the rustle of paper.

He asked, "When did you last eat?"

"Breakfast."

There was a tut of annoyance. "I've brought some food, biscuits, honey . . ." He crouched down beside her. "Can you sit up?"

She turned her head away like a petulant child. "Don't want any food."

He gave up, probably deciding to wait. His body blocked the entrance as he went outside.

Something had gone wrong. This was the man she had come to find at the inn, but he had turned into the stranger who had written that note. And she could not let that stranger touch her ever again.

She heard the sound of shovelling and scraping and she drifted off into an uneasy sleep. She awoke with a start as a hand was pushed down into the blanket, feeling for her wrist. She lay limp and unresponsive, and supposed he was taking her pulse.

She asked, her words slurring, "What have you been doing?"

"Trying to free your car. It's got to be moved. In the dark it will be a danger to other cars. It was almost submerged. Did you know that if I'd arrived just a little later . . ."

"I'd have been dead," she thought. "Why did he have to find me?"

He went to stand at the door.

"Is it still snowing?" she asked his back.

"Yes. There's a raging blizzard out there. It's dark now. We'll have to stay put until daylight." He came back and stood by her, switching on the torch again. "Are you warm enough?"

182

She did not reply, so he felt for her hand again. In the few seconds she allowed him to hold it – she snatched it away almost as soon as he made contact – the iciness of it gave him his answer. He wrapped another blanket round her. Marisa let him do it – so long as he did not touch her ... Sleep claimed her again and when she awoke she could see in the torch-light that Dirk was reclining beside her, leaning on his elbow. As soon as she stirred, he moved.

"Food, Marisa."

"No."

But he pushed his arm underneath her shoulders and supported her. "I've no hot soup, which is what you should have, but you'll have to try and manage a slice of bread spread with honey." She turned away again. He said slowly, clearly, "I've come a long way, Marisa. It took me hours to find you. This is the best I could do in the circumstances, so eat it. Please."

She took a bite from the bread he put to her lips and although the act of chewing was like rolling a giant boulder up a steep hill, she managed the whole slice. The tea, still hot, was sweet and its effect reviving. Dirk allowed her to lie back again and poured some tea for himself, using the same cup. He tossed the liquid down his throat and put the flask away.

He switched off the torch and lay down beside her. There seemed to be no covers over him, no pillow on which he could rest his head. She stirred uncomfortably and it was then that the shaking started. He was alert at once, and crouching beside her.

Her teeth chattered, her body shook, and she knew it was reaction setting in. The terrifying thing was that she could do nothing to stop it. She held her breath, clenched her fists, stiffened her body, but it was no use, the shaking went on.

Dirk whispered her name, but she could not reply. He loosened the blankets and shared them with her, his arms reaching out and pulling her to him. She wanted to pull away, but hadn't the strength.

"You've got to let me hold you, Marisa," he murmured, "to give you the warmth of my body. If you don't we'll both die – of exposure."

It was then that she felt how cold he was, and grew frightened. He mustn't die, that was not part of the plan. He must live, to go to Luella, which was what he wanted and why he had decided to divorce her, but first getting his pound of flesh by making love to her for the last time.

She let him hold her close and in the strength of his arms the shaking slowly subsided and died away, allowing tranquillity to take its place. She slept.

It must have been in the early hours that she stirred. By Dirk's deep regular breathing she guessed he was asleep, but his hold had not slackened. By the way his arms were gripping her she could almost have convinced herself that he loved her, but she had thought that before – was it only twenty-four hours ago? – and this time she was not going to be fooled into letting herself believe it again.

The tears began suddenly, taking her by surprise. They spurted out and overflowed, running down her cheeks and moistening his skin, waking him up. There was a tearing pain in her chest which was not assuaged even when the sobs racked her body. Feeling had returned at last, the stupor, the protective numbness had passed, leaving her emotions as vulnerable and defenceless as a new-born baby.

He let her cry, probably knowing it was in itself a sign of healing, that the state of deep shock which had paralysed her mind for so many hours had loosened its hold and left her, still weak and susceptible but restored to normality.

He found his handkerchief and dried her eyes and she lay passive, allowing him to do it. Then his head lifted and he listened. There was a steady pelting of rain on the roof, heralding a change in the weather pattern and the coming of the thaw. Soon the ice would melt and the temperature rise. Now the relief was his.

"Go to sleep again, my sweet," he said, his voice exultant. "In the morning the going should be easy."

Marisa stiffened at the endearment, hope raising its head like a woman listening for the long-awaited footsteps of a loved one, but it drooped again, disappointed, as she remembered how meaningless the endearment had been the last time he had used it. For a moment he must have thought she was Luella.

In the darkness, her hand lifted to his face, exploring its surface, and like someone interpreting Braille, her fingers began to read his expression. They found his forehead and touched on the furrows between his eyes. So he was frowning. They moved over his eyebrows to settle for a moment on the hardness of his cheekbone. Then down, down to discover the uncompromising rigidity of his jaw.

The fingers faltered, almost giving up, then moved tentatively, fearfully, to the last and most telling resting place, only to encounter the taut, tight line of his lips. No hope there, none at all.

"Dirk," she whispered brokenly, "oh, Dirk . . ."

She twisted her head away and tried to follow it with her body. But his hold tightened, imprisoning her, and she was trapped.

His hand lifted swiftly, catching at her chin and jerking her face towards him. "Tell me, Marisa," his voice was harsh, "do you want to divorce me?"

"No, Dirk!"

"Do you love Elwyn?"

"No, no, Dirk. I love you, so how could I –?"

His lips found hers, crushing them into stillness, compelling her to respond. He unfastened her anorak and pushed it aside. His hands caressed her body, possessive and demanding, surmounting all obstacles. He moved and, when the time was right, she found herself yielding again, willingly, ecstatically, to his passion and his desires.

Then there was silence, an exulting, breathless silence, apart from the drumming of her heart and the blood racing through her veins.

"My beloved wife," he whispered at last, "have I done enough to prove to you that I love you, that I've never stopped loving you, and never will stop loving you until the end of time?"

In response her arms reached out for him and their lips came

185

together again. And afterwards, they embraced, content and tranquil, until she spoke again. Uneasiness was invading her serenity, like the rumble of thunder from someone else's storm, unanswered questions and doubts which must be resolved.

"Dirk," she asked, confused, "Luella –?"

"We were friends, my darling, nothing more. I was the architect she employed to design her house, she was my client." His lips brushed hers. "Do you trust me, Marisa?"

"Yes, yes," she whispered.

"Then you must believe me when I say I'm telling you the truth." He murmured against her cheek, "Did you really think that after sharing your warmth and your ardour, I could honestly have contemplated spending the rest of my life making love to a block of ice?"

She laughed. "That was how Neville described her."

"And Neville was right," he murmured. "Being a man, he would understand these things."

Much later she asked, "Tell me, Dirk, why did you write that terrible note?" Her voice faltered because even now the memory hurt.

He stroked her hair. "Because, my darling, I thought it was what you wanted. After all, you'd been asking for a divorce ever since I came back."

"But only because I thought *you* wanted to be free of *me.*"

"My love, if I'd really wanted to be free of you, I could have agreed to a divorce long ago." He kissed her again. "I suppose you thought me the most unprincipled man alive to insist on my 'marital rights' once more before we finally parted?"

She nodded.

"I wanted to test you, to discover whether you still loved me, and I knew that if you did, in such circumstances you wouldn't be able to hide it. But afterwards, in the cold light of dawn, it occurred to me why you'd consented to fulfil my 'condition' on that particular night. It was because – and only because – of the drink you'd had. I tortured myself with the idea that the only way you could tolerate my touch was with a fair quantity

186

of alcohol inside you to take away the 'nasty taste'. I worked myself up into an agony of jealousy. That note was written in anger. It was only later, after I had left you and when I'd calmed down, that I began to wonder if I'd been wrong.

"I decided to see you and talk things over. I called at your flat, only to find you'd gone. I saw Mrs. Scoby. She told me you were out, hadn't come back, had gone on the moors to find an inn. I didn't believe her at first. I couldn't believe you'd been so stupid as to do such a thing in such weather. Then it occurred to me that it hadn't been – stupidity. It could have been – something else. I knew my car wouldn't make it quickly enough, so I begged the loan of this Land-Rover from a builder I knew. He agreed at once, lent me a shovel, boots and so on, so I wouldn't have to waste time going back to my flat. His wife made some flasks of tea and gave me food."

"And you arrived – just in time?"

"Yes, thank God."

There was a pause and she ventured, "Dirk, you said that night Norman and I were at your flat you'd had girl-friends. Did you mean it?"

He laughed. "You've got to know it all, haven't you? Don't you remember I also said I was the faithful type, true to the woman I loved?"

"I thought you meant Luella."

"I know you did. And I was damned if I was going to enlighten you. The way you had Elwyn hanging on to you like a shadow stuck on with adhesive –!"

She stirred in his arms. "You haven't answered my question, Dirk."

"Behaving like a possessive wife already?" He tipped up her chin with his fist. "Carry on, sweetheart, I love it. Yes, I did have girl-friends. I even tried making love to them. But it wasn't any use. Each time I kissed them I found myself imagining it was you. So I gave up. I returned from the Midlands partly at the invitation of Mr. Garner, but mainly to discover how things stood between you and Elwyn. To my chagrin, I found that nothing seemed to have changed in that quarter. When I saw the way you were going about together, I had a 'this is where I came in' sort of feeling."

"Those two nights in the hotel with you, Dirk – it was agony having you so near yet not being able to touch you."

"*You* felt that? What about me?" In the growing light of dawn he gazed into her eyes. "The second night, when I was feeling a little better, I wanted you, I wanted you passionately. If I'd asked you to come to me I knew you would have agreed, but I was convinced you would only have done it on sufferance or, worse, out of pity. Now perhaps you understand why I couldn't face a third night with you in that hotel. I had to get home, with you out of reach."

"I'm not out of reach now, darling," she whispered, and proved it.

He said, after a while, "I'm not being parted from you again. I've been without you long enough, so we're altering our style of living. When we get back, as we will some time today, you're packing a case and coming to live with me. Tomorrow we'll finish the packing. As soon as possible your tenancy of the flat will cease. Any objections?"

"None at all," she whispered, her shining eyes reflecting the morning light that was filling the rain-washed windows.

"And now," said Dirk, "I'll tell you how we're going to spend our evenings. You will sit on my knee and together we'll plan a home of our own, the first real home we've ever shared."

"Architect designed," she murmured.

"In truth, my darling, architect designed. Sensibly planned, on stable ground and built on solid, rock-hard foundations. Like our marriage from now on. Agreed, Mrs. Sterling?"

"Agreed, Mr. Sterling."

"And," he went on, his lips hovering purposefully, "we'll fill our home with all the small necessities of life."

"Small necessities that grow," she added, smiling.

Have you missed any of these . . .

Harlequin Presents..

All books listed are available at **95c each** at your local bookseller or through the Harlequin Reader Service.

TO: HARLEQUIN READER SERVICE, Dept. N 512
   M.P.O. Box 707, Niagara Falls, N.Y. 14302
   Canadian address: Stratford, Ont., Can. N5A 6W4

☐ Please send me the free Harlequin Romance Presents Catalogue.

☐ Please send me the titles checked.

I enclose $................ (No C.O.D.s). All books listed are 95c each. To help defray postage and handling cost, please add 25c.

Name ....

Address ....

City/Town ....

State/Prov. .... Postal Code..............

Have you missed any of these . . .

Harlequin Presents..

All books listed 95c

Harlequin Presents novels are available at your local bookseller, or through the Harlequin Reader Service, M.P.O. Box 707, Niagara Falls, N.Y. 14302; Canadian address: 649 Ontario St., Stratford, Ontario N5A 6W4.

Have You Missed Any of These
Harlequin Romances?